Love In A Major Key

By The Same Author

THE TRELLISED LANE
THE WEDDING PORTRAIT
THE PRACTICAL HEART

LOVE IN A MAJOR KEY

Fiona Hill

A BERKLEY MEDALLION BOOK
published by
BERKLEY PUBLISHING CORPORATION

To Harvey Klinger

Copyright © 1976, by Ellen Pall

All rights reserved

Published by arrangement with the author's agent.

All rights reserved which includes the right to reproduce this book or portions thereof in any form whatsoever. For information address

Jay Garon-Brooke Associates, Inc.
415 Central Park West #17D
New York, New York 10025

SBN 425-03019-9

BERKLEY MEDALLION BOOKS are published by
Berkley Publishing Corporation
200 Madison Avenue
New York, N.Y. 10016

BERKLEY MEDALLION BOOK ® TM 757,375

Printed in the United States of America

Berkley Medallion Edition, JANUARY, 1976

Chapter I

Lady Keyes toyed fretfully with the inkwell on her husband's desk. "I admit, Latimer," she said, "I am no more fond of the prospect than you are; but I believe my grandmother may be quite right. In fact, we ought to have done it last year."

Sir Latimer inspected his fingernails closely. "Is there no one in the neighbourhood who will answer?"

"My dear, you know there is not. I will not have my daughter marrying that horrid Reverend Blake. He is fifty if he is a day, and quite hideous as well. Though a very good man," she added conscientiously. She picked up a pen and stirred the ink with it.

"You married a neighbourhood fellow," Sir Latimer reminded his wife. "I trust it did you no harm."

"Naturally it did not; but that was because the fellow was *you*, my dear." A plaintive note entered her thin voice. "There is simply no possibility of Daphne's marrying any of our acquaintances, Latimer. To do so, she would be obliged to marry beneath herself——O! and when I think of what Lady Bryde would say to that!"

"I wish you did not stand so much in dread of your grandmother," answered her husband, for perhaps the hundredth time since their wedding-day.

Her manner growing yet more agitated, Lady Keyes stirred the ink vigorously. "But you know how she felt

1

about my mother's marriage," she said reproachfully. In a softened tone, she added, "Mine too."

Sir Latimer polished his left thumbnail with his right index finger. "I do not recall when Lady Bryde was satisfied with anything," he said, almost pettishly.

"But my dear, she is a Countess!" replied his wife, a little scandalised by his lack of respect for the venerable old lady. "She ought to know what is significant, and what is not; and she told me at Christmas that if Daphne married below her station—as Mother and I did—it would be the end of the family's position altogether. She is already disturbed over the retired life we lead, you know; she always has been." Lady Keyes peered deeply into the eddy she was making in the inkwell. "She has for ever been begging us to spend a Season in London, and we have never done so. And now with Daphne eighteen years of age, I'm afraid we simply must——O!" she broke off with a little cry. "How clumsy of me! I've spilt the ink, all over your papers—were they important, Latimer?" she asked in dismay.

"No, no," he reassured her, hurrying to blot up the widening black puddle with a handkerchief. "Margaret," he went on, when most of the ink had been soaked away, "this is not the sort of decision which can be made in an hour, don't you agree? I will consult with Clayton," he said, naming his secretary, "and you must write to Lady Bryde and ask her for particulars. When a girl ought to make her come-out, to whom she must be presented, and so on. Then we shall be able to consider this matter farther." He rose on these words and went over to the bell-cord.

"You are not going to ring for Elizabeth!" she cried.

"Certainly I am, my dear. Someone must clear up this ink or it will stain the desk permanently."

"O, but do not ask Elizabeth to do it, I beg," said she,

jumping up from her chair. "I should die of shame if a servant were to see what a mess I've created. I shall clean it up myself, Latimer," she continued, reaching out a hand to stay her husband's arm. "Really, I should prefer it," she pleaded.

"Very well, my dear," said he, smiling; "though I think you are very silly." He kissed her forehead and she went off to fetch a basin of water and some rags.

In a little while she returned and began rubbing diligently at the embarrassing spot. "Latimer," she said thoughtfully as she worked, "there is one more thing I think I ought to mention." She lowered her voice to a whisper. "It is about Clayton, you know. He is—he is . . . well, the sheeps-eyes he casts at Daphne recently are really too shocking. It would probably be just as well to remove her from his vicinity before she notices his admiration. I do not think she has as yet, but—well, it really would be too vexatious if she were to return his affection." She dipped her rag into the basin and began mopping at a new place.

"But if we go to London," said he a little anxiously, "surely Clayton will go with us? I could not do without him, Margaret; truly, I could not."

Startled, she looked up at him, sloshing the water out of her basin at the same time, so that it formed a new puddle on her husband's papers. "O my, I am sorry!" she exclaimed, applying a dry rag to this fresh disaster.

"It is nothing, my dear; nothing."

"How clumsy I am today! But if that is the case—I mean, if you think to take Clayton with us—then you will have to speak to him about it. About Daphne, I mean. Remind him of his position in the household, how grateful he should be to you—that sort of thing, my dear. Will you speak to him? Promise you will."

"I shall do whatever is necessary," he assured her,

after a brief pause. In the event, however, he did nothing at all. Lady Keyes, satisfied that she had undone as much damage as she could, left her husband's study soon after, and Sir Latimer summoned his secretary. He conferred with the younger man upon the advisability of putting his daughter on the London marriage mart, the cost of taking a town-house for the Season, the difficulties of transport to and from London and within the town itself—but not a word was said regarding Clayton's admiration for Daphne. Now the reason of this was simple: Sir Latimer Keyes was every bit as timid as his wife, and perhaps a little more so. While he did his best to conceal this fact—particularly by allowing Clayton to deal with all such frightening personages as bailiffs, and lawyers, and even the butler employed at Verchamp Park—it was nonetheless true, and the prospect of discussing with his secretary such an intimate matter as sentiment seemed quite outside the realm of possibility to him. Accordingly, he delayed fulfilling his wife's request, and in a very short time had succeeded in forgetting it altogether.

Perhaps an admonishment from him on this topic would have been without purpose anyway. Mr. Clayton might cast a veritable deluge of sheeps-eyes at Miss Daphne Keyes, but it was unlikely she would return them. He was a youngish man—twenty-nine or thirty at the most—but his countenance in no way reflected the beauty often associated with youth. On the contrary, his face was abnormally wide and ruddy, and equipped with a set of greenish eyes which protruded awkwardly therefrom. They were set close together, over a flat nose and an even flatter pair of lips. Nor did his manner reflect youth's grace. He did, it is true, have the springy step which is some times found in people who tend to be stout—but there was nothing to attract Miss Daphne's notice in this. No, Mr. Clayton was in no wise the sort of young man who plays the hero in a young girl's fancy; the best that could be said of him was that he was extremely competent, and as good-natured as one could desire. These last attributes, however, were quite enough to satisfy Sir Latimer, and he would no more have thought of journeying to London without his secretary than of reprimanding his wife, or his daughter, or—for that matter—his hounds. Sir Latimer was, as we have said, a very timid gentleman.

He had been his father's only child, and had inherited his title (Baronet) and his estate (Verchamp Park) in due course. A long line of Sir Latimer Keyes' had preceded himself and his father, and they had become shyer and more retiring with each succeeding generation. The Latimer who now stood heir to the title was, of course, the present Baronet's son, and Daphne's younger brother by a twelvemonth. Though the Baronet was in good health, and did not look to pass on his position for a good many years, both his children had already inherited, in a manner of speaking, at least one of his possessions: an acute fear of the world. Indeed, this was the family trait—as remarkable in all of them as their dark eyes and thick dark hair—and the Keyes family motto might well have been (though it was not) *Hide Thy Light under a Bushel Basket, Lest Someone Extinguish It.* Sir Latimer had married Margaret Buckwood, daughter of Lady Margaret Buckwood, daughter, in turn, of Lady Margaret Bryde, Countess of Halston. The Buckwoods had been neighbours of the Keyes' in Herefordshire, but the line had died out shortly after Miss Margaret's marriage, and all that was left of her once numerous family was Lady Keyes herself and the Countess of Halston, now five-and-seventy years of age at the very least. The Countess of Halston, elderly though she was, vehemently scorned life in the country— which she called a rude theatre, where the entertainment was fit only for groundlings—and had accordingly resided in London all her life. She frequently sneered at her grand-daughter for chusing to live retired, and—when she made her yearly Christmas visit to Verchamp—took her severely to task for imposing that life on Daphne.

"Poor Daphine" (as her great-grand-mother called her) was a "comely gal." Lady Bryde often predicted, with her accustomed shrewdness, that she would turn the heads of not a few town-bucks, could they but see her. On no occasion, however, had she offered to sponsor Daphne into Society herself; on the contrary, she freely admitted that she thought it a deadly dull task to chaperone a young girl through a whole Season, "dragging her here and there, in and out of squeezes, gabbing with all those faded dowagers while the gal thought of ways to disgrace herself. No, Margaret," she had told her grand-daughter this past Christmas, "it must be done, and the sooner the better, but you will have to do it yourself. Don't look to me, my girl! I brought your mother into Society—and those were days when Society deserved the name, which is more than I can say for these thin-blooded times; that was quite enough for me, thank you."

This was the counsel which, on the February day we have seen, moved Lady Keyes to petition her husband as she did. She herself had never even been to London, nor had ever wanted to go; Sir Latimer had made a few brief visits on business, but had hardly stirred outside the rooms of the inn he stopped at. The town-house which once belonged to the Keyes' had long since been sold, and neither Sir Latimer nor his lady had given any particular thought to the question of their daughter's marriage until Lady Bryde had become so insistent.

It may be imagined that Daphne herself lavished considerably greater attention on this question than had either of her parents, but this was not in fact the case. Indeed, she had seen so little of the world, had read so few novels and was so limited in her acquaintance, that the thought that she must some day marry had hardly occurred to her at all. At the very moment when her parents sat earnestly discussing her future, the object of their concern was absorbed with nothing more significant than the antics of her dog. Clover had appeared one day on the grounds of Verchamp Park, and had formed an instant and unshakable passion for Daphne's company. These sentiments being returned in full, the intruder was soon named and adopted. How he had happened to arrive at the Park was as mysterious a question as his ancestry, which was (as near as any one could guess) part sheep-hound and part some thing else. Anything farther than this it was impossible to determine. Whatever his antecedents, he was a sweet dog, and a very silly one. He and Daphne had walked out into the frozen February afternoon together, where Clover spent a pleasant hour chasing stones. He had just begun to tire of this pastime when he noticed a small, grey squirrel eying him, a few yards from his nose. In a trice, Clover was after him. The squirrel started and raced up an oak. Clover, his mind full of the chase, apparently forgot that dogs could not climb trees, and leapt up to pursue him. As his quarry escaped into the uppermost branches of the oak, Clover found himself perched helplessly some four feet above the earth, his paws crowded uncomfortably into the hollow formed by the trunk of the tree and its lowest branch. From this vantage point he turned doleful eyes upon his mistress, beginning to whine softly. Daphne was overcome with laughter.

"O my dear Dog," she exclaimed, "how extremely silly you look! What have you done, you great beast? What an oaf you are—a great, big, furry oaf!" Clover, evidently not finding the situation amusing, barked a single, plaintive bark. "Yes, yes, my dear; we shall get you down some how. But you must remember, another time, not to follow your nose so fast, without looking where it leads you." So saying, she held her arms out towards the animal and encouraged him to jump. "It's all right," she assured him; "you are not so very high up after all." Persuaded at last, Clover sprang from the tree on to the frozen ground, where he was received with hugs and kisses. All the way back to the house, however, Daphne scolded him gently, assuring him that she had never in her life seen any thing so large and so foolish as he.

Clearly, Miss Keyes was as little concerned with her future as might be. Her father she deemed capable of any thing necessary to be done; her mother she knew to be as warm and womanly as any daughter could wish; and her brother was the apple of her eye. Indeed, so remarkable seemed his good looks to her, she hardly noticed her own; certainly she was not disposed to dwell on them, nor to look for young men to admire her. She was fonder of her books than of her mirror, and by far more partial to riding than to conversation. She brushed her long, thick hair to keep it healthy—then tucked it away for comfort—and all her daily toilette consisted of was a vigorous scrubbing of hands and face. Accordingly, her fine skin glowed with health, her large eyes with exuberance, and her neat body was as able and energetic as any one could wish. The nearest she came to vanity was admiring her own countenance as her brother's reflected it, and flirtation was a phenomenon entirely unknown to her.

If only the same could be said of young Latimer! It can not, however; for although he enjoyed a ride as well as his sister, and frequently raced her on foot across the park, he had been a little spoiled by his sister's admiration, and was, at the age of seventeen, well on his way to becoming a cox-comb. He had been to London two years before, with his father, and had got a taste of town-life. Though the situation of Verchamp Park successfully prevented him, on his return, from becoming a full-blown fop, it must be reported that he leaned distinctly towards fashion, and yearned after well-cut coats and polished boots. Whenever possible, he procured for himself gentlemen's magazines, and studied them intently—not as intently, however, as he studied his own face in the glass. It was, perhaps, fortunate that this self-worshipping tendency of his character was countered at every step by the timidity he inherited from his parents: though he would dearly have loved to put himself forward, he was inhibited by dread of failure. Had the business of Daphne's marriage not come up, Latimer might well have outgrown his incipient dandyism without much awkwardness; but the possibility of another, and extended, visit to London excited him greatly, and he seconded his great-grandmother's advice with zeal.

"It is only fair," he said to his father, on the evening of the interview between his parents, "for Daphne's sake. A girl ordinarily makes her come-out at seventeen, you know, or even sixteen! And Daphne will not grow any younger. You ought to consider that, Father."

They were seated at the dining-table, the ladies having withdrawn some moments before. Latimer had said as much to his father on every evening since Lady Bryde's Christmas visit, so it may be imagined with what surprise and delight Sir Latimer heard his son now. On all previous occasions he had met the young man's importunities with a sage nod of the head and a promise "to take the matter into consideration." This evening, however, there was a departure from the usual proceedings. Nodding his head with extreme slowness, Sir Latimer said, "So your mother tells me. Well, I consulted with Clayton about it this afternoon, and—I don't suppose you would like to go to London with us, would you my boy?"

"Like to go to London with you!" echoed the youth. "I

should say so! That is," he amended, feeling it might be dangerous some how to show too much enthusiasm, "Daphne and I have never been apart more than a week or two, you know. I trust she would want me to go along."

"Yes; doubtless she would. But in any case, Clayton tells me——"

"Clayton's a clunch, Father," Latimer broke in impatiently. "I'm sure he found some reason why we ought not to go, but I think you might stop taking his word for Gospel."

"But he advised our going," Keyes contradicted mildly.

"He did?" said the boy, astonished.

"Indeed; he said——"

But Latimer did not wait to hear what he said. With a jubilant huzza in which there was very little that was fashionable, he leapt from his chair and leaned across the table, reaching out his hand to shake his father's heartily. "Damme if you ain't a fine fellow!" he exclaimed, and ran out of the dining parlour, straight down the long corridor to the drawing-room. "Daphne!" he shouted, bursting through the large double-doors. "Daphne! Mother! We're going to town!"

Now Sir Latimer had not really intended his words at the dining-table to be taken in quite this way. While it was true that Clayton had advised the trip, he had meant to ponder things a few days longer before making a decision. However, Latimer's news was so well received by the ladies that Keyes did not have the heart to dampen every one's excitement with sobering words. Besides, it seemed quite convenient to have the decision made for him, rather than being obliged to make it himself; so he simply submitted to his wife's embrace and his daughter's thanks, and allowed matters to follow their own course.

This they did, as matters frequently will. Within a

week, the ordinarily tranquil routine of Verchamp Park was entirely disrupted. All the family had to be fitted for new clothes, though Latimer was quick to point out the advisability of waiting to buy most of them in London itself, and the commissions given to the local seamstresses were, accordingly, kept to a minimum. Mr. Clayton rode some forty miles to visit Captain and Mrs. Butler, who were the nearest neighbours known to have visited London within recent years. From them he learned such interesting information as where to rent a house, how horses could be stabled and vehicles housed in town, and the procedure involved in acquiring vouchers for Almack's. He returned to Verchamp Park and consulted frequently with Sir Latimer, until at last matters were set in order well enough to allow him to absent himself from the family for some time. Early in March, therefore, he quitted Herefordshire and, travelling in young Latimer's curricle, arrived in London, where he set about finding suitable lodgings. The Keyes' were to follow him there as soon as he had succeeded in this object.

Lady Keyes had written to her grandmother in February, to inform her of their impending visit. For weeks she searched the post eagerly, sure of receiving a letter from Lady Bryde. None, however, arrived. This was the cause of much conjecture at Verchamp Park: had something offended the old woman? Was she sulking? Or angry with her grand-daughter? Lady Keyes wrote again, apologising for what ever it might have been (if it was anything at all) that had incurred Lady Bryde's displeasure; still, no answer was returned. She wrote repeatedly, but silence was maintained. The solution to this deep mystery, which excited more and more anxiety in Herefordshire, was in fact rather simple, and was nothing to do with the Keyes family at all (which was, very likely, what made it so puzzling to them—for of all things, we find it most difficult to believe that people occasionally determine on courses which are nothing to do with us). Lady Bryde, as was discovered later, had taken it into her head to visit the Continent, and did not therefore receive Lady Keyes' letters until her return late in March. By that time there was quite a collection of notes from Herefordshire waiting for her in Dome House, Berkeley Square; they ranged in tone from polite, to imploring, to defensive. By that time also, the Keyes' themselves were installed in London, and the letters might as well never have been written. Most of them (for the old Countess soon discovered their drift) were never read.

On the evening of the Keyes' departure, Verchamp Park bore a distinct resemblance to Bedlam. The number of questions posed by each member of the family to the others was astronomical.

"What do you think of my cravat?" Latimer demanded of his sister as he entered her bed-chamber. "I want your honest opinion; do not spare my feelings."

Daphne looked up from her packing. Her brother's chin rested uneasily on a veritable cream-puff of a cravat, a spectacular arrangement of linen which looked more like a large cumulous cloud than anything else. She hesitated for a moment.

"It is my own invention," he said proudly. "It will be called the Latimer—you know like the Mathematical, and the Oriental . . . or do you think it is too much? Perhaps it is a trifle over-done?" he went on anxiously. "Probably I look ridiculous; do I look ridiculous, Daphne? You can tell me if I look ridiculous; I won't be hurt."

Daphne took a breath, then exhaled it.

"I knew it; I knew it was too much. I'll change it—I'll do it again. But do you think it has potential, at least? No, you needn't answer that," he corrected himself, tearing at the cravat with his fingers. "I shall make another attempt; don't go away."

But Daphne did go away, to her mother's bed-chamber. "Mother," she said hesitantly, "I do not think—that is, I am afraid I am packing my trunk the wrong way. How does one do it?"

Lady Keyes had been surveying her drawers, chusing what items needed to be taken. Now she turned to her daughter. "I am sure you have done very well, my dear," she said, "but if it will make you easier, I shall come and look at it."

The two women returned to Daphne's room. The trunk sat open on the floor, its wide mouth gaping. It was nearly full. "You see," said Daphne, gesturing anxiously; "I did not know how to do it, and now——"

"But it is perfectly done," objected her mother, examining the carefully folded clothes more closely. "Or do you not have room for the rest of your things?"

"No; I mean, that is everything. But I think I must have done it incorrectly, don't you? I know nothing about packing, except that it must be done carefully, and——"

Lady Keyes hugged her daughter. "If everything is in it, you may call James and he will tie it with cord and carry it downstairs for you. I wish you would not worry so much about your ability to do things! You always do so very well."

"You are kind to say so," said Daphne, returning her mother's embrace. Then she exclaimed suddenly, "I do wish we could take Clover with us!"

"It is better not to," Lady Keyes assured her. "London is no place for a big dog. I am not sure it is a good place for us, either," she added.

On these words she hurried from the room: a few minutes later she apeeared in her husband's doorway, her countenance plainly agitated. "Latimer, my dear, I wish you will come with me for a moment. I have made a list of instructions for Elizabeth: how she is to deal with the tradesmen, when the laundering is to be done, how to reach us in London, all that sort of thing—but I am sure I have forgot an hundred details. Are you certain we ought to take Mrs. Jennings with us? She is so competent; the household runs so smoothly in her hands . . . and Elizabeth is too young, surely, to take her place."

"But we will need a housekeeper in London, you know," he answered doubtfully. "It was Clayton who suggested Elizabeth; I am sure she is capable of new duties, if Clayton says so."

"Yes . . . but so much responsibility! Please do come and look at my list. I *know* I have left something out."

"In a moment," he agreed. "But first, tell me something. I am afraid—it occurs to me that perhaps we ought not to be taking Latimer with us? I have heard a great deal about how town-life affects a growing boy; perhaps we will do better to leave him at home."

And so the evening was engulfed in questions, doubts and fears. When night came at last hardly a soul slept, so preyed upon were they by their various worries. When the family met at breakfast the next morning, each face bore the tell-tale traces of sleeplessness: heavy-lidded eyes, and pale complexions. It was a relief to every one to enter the Keyes' coach at last; by ten o'clock, for better or for worse, they were on their way to London.

On a crisp March morning some few days later, the Countess of Halston was seated in her drawing-room endeavouring to make some sense of the correspondence which had accumulated at Dome House during her two-months' absence. When she heard her butler's quiet knock at the door, she looked up, pleased at the interruption in her tedious work, and barked a shrill "Come in." Hastings entered bearing a silver tray, upon which lay a card inscribed "Anthony Graves, Lord Houghton." Lady Bryde snorted and drew back her thin lips in a sage smile. "I am at home," she informed the butler, inclining her head slightly. When he had gone through the doors again, she touched her elaborate coiffure with a wrinkled hand, and drew forth a side-curl to make it a little more prominent. "Not," she assured herself, "that it makes the least bit of difference; but Anthony is a shameless gossip, and it never does to look unwell."

Lord Houghton entered a few moments later. As Lady Bryde did not rise to meet him, he crossed the room to the tufted-velvet chair in which she sat and bowed deeply; to the Countess' deep satisfaction, he knelt before her and took her hand, kissing it and murmuring, "Margaret! As lovely as ever!"

"I declare," she remarked in response; "when you do that I can almost hear your knees creak, Anthony. Get up off the floor, you silly old fool, and tell me which nonsense you've been keeping busy with."

If Lord Houghton was injured by these words, he did not show it. His faded blue eyes twinkled as he rose, with some difficulty, and took a seat near her ladyship.

"By God, you *are* creaking!" she exclaimed. "Never tell me you've taken to wearing corsets, Tony!"

"The sad truth," he admitted, a rueful grin lighting up his wrinkled countenance. "The years, my dear . . . they do not sit so lightly upon me as they do on you."

"Faugh!" said she. "I daresay you'll be driving a perch-phaeton, next thing we know, and talking about things being 'all the crack,' and 'cutting a dash about town.' The trouble with you is not old age, dear sir; the trouble with you is perennial infancy."

"A second childhood, perhaps?" he suggested humbly.

"You always were a child."

"How sorrowful it is, Margaret! Now that I am ripe enough to appreciate your beauty as it ought to be appreciated, I am too old to honour it properly. That is the essence of age, my dear: desire is behind us; we are left with only the desire to desire."

"You're an old fool," she repeated, cackling fondly.

"But Margaret," he began earnestly, "in all honesty, you look——"

"Spare me your honesty!" she interrupted, raising a dry, fragile hand. "I gave up honesty years ago—particularly with regard to my looks. Tell me the truth and you cannot help but insult me; and I never was partial to insults. At six-and-seventy, a neat lie is all I ask."

The Countess was a little severe in her self-criticisms. While it was true that she was old, that her cheeks had lost their colour and her lips their fullness, it was equally true that her countenance, when animated, was still pleasant to look upon. She had a snowy beauty, and though time had robbed her of youth's crimson and fire, she still sparkled with energetic interest. Her noble carriage gave her an air of elegance which never deserted her, and the powdered peruke which she insisted on wearing—though it had long since gone out of fashion—imparted to her appearance something like the beauty of fine antique objects, curios out of a bygone era. Lord Houghton exaggerated, of course—but not too much.

"You are simply beautiful, my dear," he said. "No longer a rose, perhaps, but at least a lily. And now, since I see you are about to reprimand me for this flattery, I shall skilfully turn the conversation. I am pleased to announce, my Lady, that even at my advanced age, I have a new vice, and therefore a new sin to confess."

"Anthony!" she cried, leaning forward with a smile. "This is fascinating! Do tell me. I hope it is an original sin, and not a stale one."

"Under the circumstances, Margaret, I think I have done rather well. I have taken," he went on proudly, "to Sloth."

"Sloth! O Anthony, this is a disappointment! Surely you can think of something better than that?"

"But my dear, it is not *what* is done, so much as the *way* it is done. Or rather, not done. I have become if I may say so, an absolute artist of apathy—a lord of lethargy—a technician of torpor! I assure you, I do positively nothing at all; and, what is more, I do it all day."

"Is that all you came to say?" she inquired unkindly.

"Margaret, you wound me."

At this juncture, their conversation was interrupted by a knock at the door, followed immediately by Hastings, who entered this time with a brief note. The direction on the letter was unfamiliar to her Ladyship, and she tore it open with faint curiosity. She scanned it hurriedly and broke out, presently, in long peals of dry laughter. "O dear Heavens!" she exclaimed, wiping an eye which had begun to tear; "O my Lord, this is too amusing!" Again her laughter overtook her and she could not speak. When at last her mirth had subsided some what, she waved the letter at Lord Houghton and said in explanation: "It is from my grand-daughter, Anthony; she and her family are in London, and they've taken a house——O dear!" she cried, cackling helplessly again. "they've taken a house in Marylebone!"

Chapter II

"Shall I come with you, Margaret?" Lord Houghton asked, when Lady Bryde had rung for Hastings and given orders for her carriage to be prepared immediately.

"As you like," she returned diffidently. "It is certain to be amusing . . . but will it not interfere with your programme of lethargy? A visit to Marylebone may be quite an effort."

"For love of you, my dear, I will give up even my art."

"That is very poor policy, as I am sure you know. Never give up any thing for love: that has always been my motto. The last time I lifted a finger to accommodate a man was when I was sixteen, sir, and I have lived a very happy life."

"It is different for a woman," he murmured, accepting his hat and stick from Hastings.

"Not so different as you imagine," she said; "but never mind. Were everyone to discover the secrets I have discovered, I should not feel so privileged. Hastings," she added, "please ask Goodbody to fetch my redingote and send it down here—the green one, with the black frogs."

"Very well, my Lady," said he, turning.

"Of all men in the world," said Lady Bryde, as the butler vanished, "Hastings is my favourite."

"Not myself?" cried Houghton.

"I am never partial to any one who is not my social

inferior," she replied. "It is much too dangerous. In fact, I always liked Hastings better than I did Halston," she mused to herself. "Though naturally, I never told either of them. Shall we be on our way?" she invited, as Hastings returned with her cloak.

A short time later, the Countess' lozenged coach swept up before an address in Marylebone and stopped. The coachman opening the door, Lady Bryde sprang out and tripped lightly down the newly-painted carriage steps. A slight shudder shook her narrow shoulders as she surveyed the house before her. She spoke in a harsh whisper to Lord Houghton, who was still in the act of climbing out, rather gingerly, of the carriage. "I feel," she said, "as if I had stepped barefoot into a patch of mushrooms. If there is one vulgar thing I abhor more than another, it is new brick. I have never seen any thing quite so . . ." she paused, summoning up the appropriate word.

A considerable amount of new brick was now in her view. The house which Clayton had selected—after much deliberation—was no more than five years old; the neighbouring buildings, too, appeared to have been constructed recently. In fact, the whole neighbourhood of Marylebone had been recommended to him by Captain Butler as being one of the newest and cleanest in London. The fact that those very elements were what made Marylebone hopelessly unfashionable never occurred to the good secretary, and the accents of loathing with which Lady Bryde now uttered the single word, "bourgeois," would have surprised him no end. "Come, my dear," said she, placing a frail hand on Anthony's arm. "We must not waste a moment."

James, who had accompanied the family to London, opened to the Countess and recognized her at once. "Your Ladyship," he said, bowing and preparing to receive her wraps.

"Never mind that now," she snapped, advancing into the tiny hall, Lord Houghton close behind her. "Where is my grand-daughter?" she demanded.

"Sir Latimer and Lady Keyes are both from home, just at present Madam. I believe they walked out into the neighbourhood."

"Then let us pray nobody of importance sees them," she replied. "Not likely to in this place, any how. Fetch Daphne to me."

James bowed. "If your Ladyship will please to wait in here?" he said, indicating a large parlour of awkward proportions, which stood to the right of the hallway. The visitors went in and seated themselves. The room had been decorated in the Egyptian motif which was then so modish; Lady Bryde inspected it critically from the low, nearly cushionless bench on which she had been obliged to sit.

"Inelegant and comfortless," she pronounced at last.

"Not what you and I are used to, perhaps," Lord Houghton began mildly, "but——"

"You are about to read me a sermon on the advisability of changing with the times," she interrupted. "Do not, please. I have enough to do to stay what I am, without bothering my head about adjustments. Besides, it is the duty of the elderly to be conservative. If there were no old-guard, there could be no reaction, and consequently no progress. Daphne!" she said, presenting a cheek to her great-grand-daughter as she entered the parlour. "I see your parents have learnt the London adage, that everything is to be got with money. It isn't true, you know."

"I beg your pardon, ma'am?" said Daphne, frankly puzzled. She was looking charmingly in a pale blue day-dress, with slippers of the same shade. Her long, thick plaits had been looped up on either side of her head, and blue ribands brushed her cheeks gently.

"Never mind, gal," said Lady Bryde, unbuttoning her redingote at last. "Tell James to take this from me, and have him bring us some ratafia. Do you care to take any thing?" she inquired of Lord Houghton.

"No, my dear; but I wish you will present me to this lovely lady."

"O, indeed," she said. She nodded curtly to Daphne. "Go on, run and fetch James. When you return I shall introduce you to your first London gentleman."

Daphne did as she was told and was back presently. "Mrs. Jennings will bring your ratafia in a moment, Madam," said James to the Countess, as he helped her off with her coat and disappeared discreetly.

"Daphne," said the Countess, "this gentleman is Anthony Graves, Lord Houghton. He has been a gossip-monger and a notorious flirt for well over fifty years. Never tell him any thing, my dear, and never believe a word he says. Anthony, this is my great-grand-daughter, Miss Keyes."

Daphne courtesied with natural grace to Houghton, who took her hand directly. "What a flower you are!" he exclaimed. "The image of Margaret in her youth."

"I am—very pleased to make your acquaintance," said she.

"You could not be so pleased as I am to make yours, Miss Keyes," he said. "If only I were fifty years younger! Even forty would suffice."

This was Daphne's first encounter with flattery. For a moment she stood silent, thinking hard. "But if you were, sir," she answered at last, "I should perhaps never have met you at all; for I think you would not be so well acquainted with my great-grandmother."

"Brava!" cried the Countess, clapping her hands. "I see you will have no trouble with the bucks you are sure to meet. Come and kiss me again, Daphne," she said.

Lord Houghton relinquishing her hand, the young woman obliged her.

"So you are glad to be in London, eh girl?" asked Lady Bryde.

"I am, ma'am."

"And you think, no doubt, that your parents have fixed you in a pretty fine house?"

"It seems so," said Daphne.

" 'One false step is ne'er retrieved,' " murmured her Ladyship, " 'Nor all that glisters, gold.' My dear," she said in a louder tone, "the sad truth is, that you could not be more unfortunately lodged—no, not if you were fixed in Bridewell."

"Indeed, ma'am?" cried Daphne, astonished.

"Certainly not. At least in gaol there would be little chance of your meeting with any of the *ton*. Here, however . . . well, who knows but what some one might blunder into Marylebone?"

"Marylebone is a—a low place, then?" she hazarded.

"It is worse than a low place, my dear: it is a middle place. One may be resurrected from poverty, Daphne, even from squalor; but no phoenix ever rose from the ranks of the bourgeoisie. We must remove you, and your—I am sure, well-meaning—family at once."

"But we have only just settled here! Surely, where one lives cannot be so important as that? Captain Butler told us——"

"Ah, so he is the villain, is he?" Lady Bryde interrupted. "I met him at Christmas," she explained to Anthony; "a climbing sort of fellow. No doubt it is his fondest wish to own a house in Marylebone. However, it will not answer for you, Daphne."

"I suppose not; that is, if you are quite certain . . ."

"I am more than certain, my dear. I am right. And now

I think I hear your parents coming in. Is your brother at home?"

"Yes; I think he is upstairs."

"Then go and fetch him, please. I see it is time I delivered a lecture on the topic of town-life. You may as well all be present."

Daphne rose with a brief courtesy and turned to quit the room. "O, and one more thing, my dear," added the Countess. "See if you cannot find your Mr. Clayton. I know your father believes nothing these days until he has heard it from Mr. Clayton's lips."

In a few minutes the household had been assembled in the parlour. Lord Houghton was introduced all round, and Lady Bryde prepared to hold forth. "My good people," she began, her hands folded firmly in her lap, "the city of London is like no other city in the world. In it, you will find, a number of very odd customs obtain. They will seem to you peculiar; they will seem to you arbitrary; at times, they may even seem not worth regarding." Here she paused to fix her audience with a stern gaze. "Believe me I pray: they *are* worth regarding. Learn them. Follow them. If necessary, do not even attempt to understand them. Simply ape them, foolish though they may be, as if your lives depended on it. They do. Am I understood?" she inquired. No one spoke. "I trust I am. Now, if I were to try to catalogue all of these customs to you, we should be here till evening. Besides, you would undoubtedly forget more than you remembered. Instead, I shall give you certain rules of thumb; you may rest assured of the utter truth of every thing I am about to tell you. Are you all quite ready?" Again, no one answered. "Very well, then. The first thing you must do is to vacate this house immediately. If possible, never even drive through Marylebone again. You will take a house in Grosvenor

Square, if we can find one. If not, an hundred places will be better than where we are now. Second: do not speak to strangers. Do not approach any one to whom I have not introduced you. If you feel overwhelmingly drawn to converse with some one, ask me first. I will determine whether it is a person with whom you should be acquainted. Master Latimer, you especially must take note of this: as wealthy and as gullible as you are, certain men will be positively drooling to take you into low company and make a cake of you. Is that clear?"

"Very clear," said Latimer, feeling unduly chastened.

"Good. The third and last rule, then, is never to do any thing first. Do not attempt to take the initiative. Do not endeavour to set a fashion. Do not pick up a fork, do not reach for a glass, until at least three other people have done so. Do not, Daphne, accept a dance until other couples are on the floor. Do not, Latimer, invite a young lady in to supper until two or three parties have preceded you. Do not remark upon any thing which has not already been remarked upon. Do not, in short, do any thing which might possibly be called original. It is certain to be the death of you. Have I made my point?"

The company nodded mutely.

"Excellent. The Keyes' will very soon be spoken of as the very best London families are spoken of; which is to say, not spoken of at all. Believe me, that is the highest praise one may aspire to. And now, Mr. Clayton, I believe you and I must have a brief tête-à-tête on the subject of residences. The rest of you will probably wish to start packing." With a grave inclination of the head, she dismissed the assembled party. A short time later she and Lord Houghton took their leave, abjuring the Keyes family as they went not to stir out of their present abode until they had a better direction to return to. Mr. Clayton issued from the house soon after, to attend to her Ladyship's instructions.

Within three days, the family had been reestablished intact in a small but pleasant house near Grosvenor Square. It was called Finchley House, probably from the circumstance of some one named Finchley having built it, though no one seemed to know for certain. The interior was, Lady Bryde noted with approval, decorated in the style which had been current during her early youth: there was a great deal of polished mahogany, all the draperies were rich and heavy, and nearly everything was panel-gilt. A large tapestry, representing Andromache exiled among the Greeks, had been hung in the dining-parlour, and she gazed pensively across the table at a number of sombre oil-paintings. The walls everywhere, in fact, were hung with such paintings, and Daphne discovered to her dismay that her bed-chamber was graced with a portrait of a quite hideous old man, who stared at her alarmingly.

When, a se'ennight later, the family assembled once more, they did so in the oak-panelled drawing-room. It was twilight; long blue shadows washed the polished wood floor. Darkness was falling quickly; Daphne observed the reflection of the lamp beside her become brighter and brighter on the panes of the tall windows, until at last Mrs. Jennings came in and untied the long velvet draperies that covered them at night. She was seated, wearing a white gown with lace ruffles at the tight wrists, on a gilt-wood settee upholstered with shiny blue-and-white brocade. Her hair, drawn smooth over her temples, had been gathered under her ears and woven into a series of long, thin plaits, which had then been caught up and looped into circles. With an unconscious motion, she smoothed several of the tiny pleats of muslin which adorned the bodice of her dress and touched an uneasy finger to one of the ornamental bone buttons which ran down its center. Her mother and brother were with her, but her father was no where to be seen.

"Mamma," said Latimer at last, jumping up from the gilt-wood chair which matched the settee on which Daphne was seated, "perhaps you'd better go and fetch him. It won't do to be late to our very first soirée. Besides," he added a bit slyly, "my great-grandmother will be watching for us—you may depend upon it. She won't like our being tardy." He began to pace up and down the drawing-room, his shiny high-lows tapping an impatient tattoo on the floor-boards. He had insisted on wearing trousers—against his mother's better judgement—and he looked very odd to his sister, who was accustomed to see him in breeches. His tone was unusually low; this was because of the fact that his cravat rose almost to his chin, and he could not open his mouth fully without imperilling its careful folds. Lord Houghton had commended the young man to the care of his own tailor, and the clothing he now wore represented the compromises that had been struck between them. Master Latimer insisted on cutting a dash; his tailor assured him that the best way to do that was to dress in unstartling garments, yet which fitted superbly. Thus it was that Latimer's sky-blue coat encircled his waist to perfection—but from under this, instead of the white waist-coat which he should have worn, a pair of pink-and-blue striped points peeped out. Looking at him thoughtfully, Daphne was rather relieved that the only colour she was permitted to wear was white.

"Your father is not accustomed to going out in Society," Lady Keyes now answered mildly. "We must give him time."

"Time! The dancing will be all done with by the time we arrive," cried Latimer. Then, observing the injured look in his mother's eyes, he added, "I beg your pardon, Mamma. I didn't mean to jump at you; it's only that—I suppose I'm a bit agitated." He looked at his sister curiously. "Aren't you the least bit excited, Daph? You look as cool as ice."

"Of course I am excited, my dear—but Madame Jardinière cautioned me that if I fretted, I would be certain to stain my gown, or to twist the muslin and crumple it. She said I must be calm." A smile lit her lips. Madame Jardinière was the French dress-maker to whose establishment Lady Bryde had sent her. "She pronounced calm as though it had two L's in it: callm, or callum. It was quite droll."

"How does she expect you to dance?" asked Latimer.

"I do not know," mused Daphne. "I do not believe she meant for me to dance at all—merely to sit, or stand, and look *jolie*."

"Doing it a bit too brown, I think," said her brother.

"What does that mean?" Lady Keyes inquired.

"O! It is a cant expression. I learnt it from an ostler."

"That is an interesting place to learn vocabulary," his mother commented, with not the least severity of tone.

"Yes . . . well, you two had better not use it, but it is quite all right for me. Mamma, where *is* Father?"

Before Lady Keyes had time to answer, Sir Latimer's step was heard on the stair-case, and the doors to the drawing-room opened. "Good-evening," said he; "every one ready?" Sir Latimer was wearing stockinette pantaloons, black, with the usual white waist-coat and a coat of muted blue. His son noted with disapprobation that his stock had been tied with as little fuss as possible. Even more disheartening was the forest-green enamelled snuff-box which Sir Latimer now drew nervously from his pocket.

"You aren't going to bring that along!" the youth

exclaimed involuntarily, as his father took a pinch of snuff with a slightly trembling hand.

"And why not, may I ask?"

"It is—so ordinary! So countrified!"

"But I am from the country," the Baronet protested.

"That is nothing to do with it!" cried Latimer. "Sir," he added, rather too late.

"And what shall I do? Go without snuff the whole evening?"

"Yes . . . I mean, no, of course not. But—O, blast it all, let us be off or we shall never get there at all."

"My idea precisely," said his father. "I think the coach is waiting. Margaret—" he said, offering an arm to his wife. The two children descended to the ground floor behind their parents.

They had never met their hostess, Lady Mufftow, before. Lady Bryde had arranged for the Keyes' to be invited, thinking that one of Drusilla Mufftow's dreary little soirées would be an appropriate introduction to what is some times called the brilliant social whirl of the *ton*. "At least," the Countess remarked to Lord Houghton, "if they disgrace themselves there, no one of interest will see them. No one, that is, except ourselves."

"Except yourself, my dear," Lord Houghton had corrected. "I have no intention of going."

"But Anthony, I shall die of tedium!"

"Nonsense, Margaret. Tedium does not curtail life; it prolongs it. For my part, I shall be at White's. If you do feel your vitality ebbing away from you, you may send a note round to me there."

"Anthony, I consider this really too unkind," Lady Bryde had said. However, nothing could move the old gentleman, and the Countess, when her carriage rolled up to Lady Mufftow's door on the evening in question, emerged alone.

"Good-evening, Drusilla," she said, when she reached the large drawing-room in which the company was gathering. "You ought to do some thing about all those ghastly stairs," she added, referring to the marble double-staircase which led from the ground to the first floor; "there is no question but what they get longer with every passing year."

She paused to look about her while Lady Mufftow made polite inquiries. "I am very well, thank you," she said in answer to these. "You look quite pinched. I suppose you have been drinking vinegar again. I assure you, it does you no good."

Lady Mufftow, a rather short woman inclined to plumpness, was addicted to the idea of losing weight. Her most recent regime consisted of a good deal of vinegar and very little of any thing else. It had, indeed, succeeded in reducing some of her bulk; however, her cheeks were very pale indeed, and she did not look at all happy. She wore a high turban, which was meant to elongate her squat figure; its effect, unfortunately, was rather to dwarf her, since it was hopelessly out of proportion with the rest of her person. Still, her faded eyes brightened at the mention of vinegar, and she began to talk enthusiastically about the success of her diet.

The Countess interrupted her in a very few minutes. "Drusilla," she said, "you must help me to understand some thing. Now it is generally agreed, among good society, that one does not talk about food. The entire business of eating, in fact, is felt to be a rather unpleasant affair, discussion of which, moreover, is as needless as it is distasteful. Why is it, then, that whenever a person restricts his diet, or consumes particularly nasty things, the question of nourishment suddenly appears to him to be the most fascinating, irresistible topic of conversation?" Lady Mufftow, quite understandably, was silent. "When you have answered that for me, my dear, you may tell me if my grand-daughter has arrived yet."

"Margaret," said Lady Mufftow at last, "I do not know how you contrive it. Every other word from your lips is a criticism; and yet one likes you so extremely!" She sighed a quiet little sigh. "I have not seen any of the Keyes family," she went on. "If they are come, I did not hear them announced."

"No, I do not see them any where. I wonder if they were delayed? It is very vexatious of them; I particularly came late myself, so that I should not be obliged to wait for them. I detest soirées, you know; one is for ever being buffeted about, and the hum of conversation generally puts me to sleep. O dear, now you will think I have been rude, Drusilla. You know I do not mean any thing by it."

She pressed her hostess' hand hastily and went off towards the thick of the crowd. There was quite a number of people already present; what Lady Mufftow described as a quiet evening did not coincide with the Countess' notion of one. To amuse herself, she counted the company, and found there were some twenty couples, most of whom fell into the tenebrous category of middle-age. A good number were young, however, and there were two women who had been in London the year she herself had made her come-out. She addressed one of these now.

"Letitia, my dear, so very good to see you. I am well, thank you, and so are you. Now that we have dispensed with that, do tell me where that music is coming from. Do you know?" The strains to which Lady Bryde alluded could be heard clearly above the murmur of voices. It was piano forte music, and was played with great feeling, the clear notes dropping like rain from the instrument.

" I believe the player is in the ball-room," said Letitia, a little annoyed with her old friend for having broke into a discussion of some interesting bit of scandal. "His name is Christian Livingston, I think; the Viscountess Dedham employed him last week, to play at that ridiculous rout party she gave. Were you there?"

But Lady Bryde did not answer. Her elegant, powdered head inclined to one side, she was listening intently to the music. It was a sonata; time after time the brief theme recurred, now emphasized, now reversed: on each occasion of its reappearance, it gained new meaning, added nuance. Eventually, she began to drift towards the doors of the drawing-room; her progress was stopped, however, by the announcement of the Keyes family. She went to meet them and surveyed them coolly.

"Not too bad," she pronounced at last. "Latimer, never wear that waist-coat again. I presume you met Lady Mufftow?"

"Yes, at the door, Grandmamma," Lady Keyes replied. "She seemed very gracious."

"She is not," the Countess replied. "She is kind-hearted. There is a difference, my dear; it has to do with style. To be gracious, one must have countenance. Any one at all may be kind-hearted. Now I suggest, Daphne, that you come with me. I shall introduce you to a girl who made her come-out last season. Her name is India, and I believe she is quite sweet, but I must caution you: a girl who has been out for a full year and has not yet been offered for frequently becomes rather hard. Do as she does, but pay no attention to what she says. Her manner is perfect; her notions are likely to be silly, or worse. Latimer, you may as well come with us. India has a brother about your age." So saying, she shepherded the two young people across the room, taking a moment first to remind their parents to speak to no one until she had returned to introduce them properly. She bowed slightly and murmured a few words of greeting to several people, all the time efficiently propelling her great-grandchildren across the room to where India Ballard and her brother, William, were standing.

Her introductions were perfunctory in the extreme. In effect, she simply pushed the young people together, saying their names curtly and abjuring them to enjoy the evening. After that she went away, leaving Daphne and Latimer entirely at a loss for what to do. It occurred to Daphne to speak, but she remembered Lady Bryde's warning that she was not to initiate anything. Latimer, his chin held uncomfortably high above his cravat, stared at his sister. Just when the silence among them became positively unbearable, India Ballard spoke. "I suppose you have come here to find a husband," she said to Daphne. "You will discover it is not nearly as simple a matter as you think."

Chapter III

Daphne hesitated for a moment, her fingers reaching involuntarily for the bone-buttons on her bodice. "If that is so," she answered finally, with half a smile, "then I shall be obliged to return home without one. It is not so very significant after all. At least we shall have seen London."

William Ballard returned her smile with a braver one and bowed slightly as he spoke. "I think Miss Keyes will have no difficulty in finding suitors. Her difficulties will be in chusing among them."

Daphne met his gaze unwillingly. He was about twenty-three years old, narrow-shouldered and high-waisted. Fair-haired and light-complected, his features appeared to have been pinched with admirable thrift from his slightly freckled face. A narrow nose, a pair of ungenerous lips, a sharp chin and wide, shallowly-set eyes presented themselves to Daphne's troubled glance. The eyes, green like his sister's, were lighted now with a faint, electrical amusement. "You are kind to say so, sir," she replied; "but if your sister has found London thin of agreeable suitors, I am sure I must discover it to be so as well."

India Ballard smiled at this and extended an impulsive hand to Daphne. "You must not mind William, you know. He is an incorrigible flatterer. Still," she added, sighing, "he is quite right. You are prettier than I am, and will no doubt have an easier time of it. Is this your first visit to London, then?" She withdrew her pale hand from Daphne's after giving it a reassuring squeeze. She resembled her brother very closely, though the slightness of his traits became her some what better. She was very near to him in stature, which meant she was a bit tall for a woman, and though her figure was painfully stick-like, she held herself well up and was by no means unpleasant to look upon. Daphne felt herself warming to the older girl.

"It is indeed," she said. "Latimer has been before, and so has my father, but my mother and I are entirely uninitiated. We have already committed some gross improprieties," she confided, adding, "quite without meaning to, of course."

"Goodness!" cried India, laughing. "And what were they?"

"My sister exaggerates," Latimer interrupted. "In truth, they were only very small improprieties, and they have since been corrected. My great-grandmother, Lady Bryde, is taking care that we do not repeat them."

"You intrigue me," India responded, "but I will not press you. It must be quite daunting to have Lady Bryde for a chaperon. I am sure she frightens me to death."

"O, she is not so bad as that," Daphne reassured her. "Though I must admit, she has intimidated me to the point where I can scarcely say or do any thing without long and careful consideration. I daresay I am not difficult to intimidate," she concluded, with a rueful smile.

"Then you must learn to be bolder," William informed her. "The gentlemen of London are quick to turn a lady's timidity to good account—or at least," he added, in an undertone to Latimer, "what they consider to be good account."

"Why don't you go off and fetch us some punch?" said India to her brother, rather bluntly. "I am sure Miss Keyes must be thirsty. Such a crowd!" She fanned herself emphatically with a tiny silver-and-ivory fan.

"India!" cried William in a plaintive voice, "I protest, you ought not to——" Then, thinking better of it, he merely bowed and invited Latimer to join him on his errand. The women remained alone in the large drawing-room while the two young men went off to discover the punch-bowl.

As soon as they had gone, India turned to Daphne and whispered excitedly, "Come with me into the ball-room, won't you? I have been aching since we arrived to get close to the pianoforte, but William insisted I stay here and attempt to attract some notice from the gentlemen." She took Miss Keyes' hand and began to lead her from the room. "Do you care for music at all? I simply adore it!"

"Yes, I am very fond of it," Daphne answered, as they threaded their way towards the ball-room, "but I do not play at all well."

"Perhaps you sing, then?"

"Abominably," Daphne confessed.

"I dote on singing," said the elder girl. "William has a very pleasant voice too, when one can persuade him to be serious and use it properly. We often sing duets; you must come and join us. I am sure your voice cannot be so hopeless as you say."

Daphne was about to protest that it was—and, in truth, it was—when they arrived at the doors to the ball-room. Except for the pianofortist, it was empty. Miss Ballard checked in the door-way and held up a cautionary hand to her companion. It was unnecessary. The music, heard clearly now, was irresistibly charming. Deep, mellow notes rolled out of the bass, complemented continually by the thin, brittle warbling of the treble. Both young women caught their breath and listened, spell-bound.

Even if they had spoken, the player would not have

noticed them. Absorbed in his music, he was as distant from his surroundings as could be. His back, long and perfectly straight, scarcely moved at all; the whole of his being seemed concentrated in his arms and hands, which rose and fell with enormous power, always gracefully controlled. He appeared to be some seven- or eight-and-twenty years of age; when he left the key-board, he stood just under six feet tall. Now, however, he sat at the instrument, his blond head held upright over broad, straight shoulders. The gleaming, waveless hair had become unkempt as he played; a few strands were falling diagonally across the clear, heedless brow. He sat in profile to the women, his bronze skin and large green eyes shining in the light of the candles which illuminated the keys. The eyes, alive with a ferocious intensity, seemed fixed on nothing. All his thought and strength were gathered in the long, curved fingers, perfectly articulated and unadorned by any ring, which struck the black and white keys with unerring, unhesitating precision. As these delivered and repeated the final, crashing chords of the sonata, an almost imperceptible quiver could be discerned in his full, cleanly-curved mouth, and the sensuous crimson lips blushed a shade deeper. While the last vibrations of music died away, he removed his hands from the pianoforte and dropped them in his lap, tossing his head back as he did so to reclaim the straying golden hair. The musculature beneath his smooth, straight features relaxed visibly, and he stretched his hands out slowly, rubbing his wrists.

When the last strains had been inaudible for some fifteen seconds, India Ballard could no longer resist applauding. She clapped her hands together and cried, "It is so beautiful; Miss Keyes, is it not unbelievably beautiful?"

"It is," she agreed in a low tone. Christian Livingston,

startled to find himself with an audience, had turned round and now regarded the young women curiously. He divided his glance evenly between them, and a faintly sardonic expression crept into his countenance, his forehead and nostrils regaining their former tension.

"I am delighted to hear it pleases you," he said, his voice clear and remarkably toneless. "Hadn't you better return to the drawing-room, though?" he inquired.

As he seemed to be addressing India, it was she who answered. "I am terribly sorry if we disturbed you," she said with composure. "I am sure it never occurred to me that we might."

"O!" he responded, the colour of his eyes deepening to a jade-green, "it is not for my sake but for yours that I suggest it. I think you must be better amused there; that is all."

"On the contrary, sir," she replied. "The attractiveness of mere talk can be nothing to the pleasure of music."

"Indeed?" said he, with a smile. He did not appear to believe her. "And you?" he asked, directing his gaze towards Daphne. "Do you share the opinion of your friend?"

"I do, Mr.——" she faltered.

"Livingston," he supplied. "You see, I do not ask your names, for I think I have no right to know them. However, a cat may look at a king. It has been very pleasant speaking with you both, but if you will pardon me, I will return to my work. Lady Mufftow will be wondering what sort of ramshackle fellow she engaged."

"Of course," said Daphne. She was completely at a loss to understand the unmistakable hardness of his tone; so far as she knew, he had no cause to take her or her companion in dislike. Her disposition was not such, however, as to encourage her to challenge him, and setting a hand on India's arm, she turned to leave the ball-room.

"I wonder why he said that—about cats and kings, you know," whispered Miss Ballard as they returned to the drawing-room.

Daphne merely shook her head in answer. "Our brothers will be asking themselves where we are," she said, after a moment. "We must hurry and find them."

This was accomplished without much difficulty, and the evening passed away without further incident. Neither girl mentioned their conversation with the pianofortist, and when the time came for dancing, Daphne hung about the walls as much as possible to avoid a second exchange with him—even an exchange of glances. She was not permitted to dance any way, she learned from India, until she had made her come-out. The music which Mr. Livingston supplied for the dancers was familiar and uninspired; he played it competently but without interest, and a dull shadow veiled his eyes.

Daphne's come-out was being arranged for her by Lady Bryde. The Countess would have preferred to have had nothing at all to do with it, but her grand-daughter's total bewilderment as to what needed to be done soon convinced her that she had best contrive it herself. Finchley House did not have a ball-room any way, and Lady Bryde insisted on seeing her great-grand-daughter brought out in the most correct and sumptuous style. Consequently the large saloons at Dome House were submitted to a vigorous round of dusting and polishing; the great chandelier which hung over the ball-room was relieved, for the first time in years, of the brown Holland which shrouded it, and its crystal drops were rubbed till they shone. The walls of the ball-room had been covered with red-and-white paper, the white being creamy and smooth, the red of raised velvet. It was designed in a floral pattern shot through with vertical stripes, and this motif was repeated in the long brocaded curtains which hung at the many windows and flanked the

French doors. These doors opened on to a terrace, and Lady Bryde arranged for the wrought-iron railings round it to be garlanded with red and white roses, masses of which were also distributed about the interior of the room. The drawing-room, being predominantly blue, was filled with hyacinths, and the Green Saloon, converted to a supper-room, was heaped with jonquils. Every available sconce was supplied with tall, white candles, and by the time Daphne arrived from the house in Grosvenor Square, all of these had been lighted.

Lady Bryde had invited simply every one whose acquaintance might be of value to her great-grand-daughter. This, it turned out, meant about four hundred people, the cream of London Society; very few of the gentlemen were not to be found among the pages of the Peerage. Daphne, of course, was not consulted about any thing, and least of all when the invitations went out. When the responses were returned, Lady Bryde discovered—without much surprise, but with a little satisfaction—that nearly all of them had been accepted. It was the first time since she had been widowed, fifteen years before, that she had entertained on a scale which even approached this; no one, among the *ton,* wished to be absent. The Countess had been a celebrated hostess in her day, and Daphne's come-out promised to be an extraordinary event.

A corner of the ball-room had been reserved to the musicians. In it stood an enormous pianoforte of rich, gleaming rose-wood, and several chairs and music-stands for the violinists. The violinists, who arrived shortly after Daphne herself, were men of middle-age, short and greasy-collared. Two of them were brothers; the third, a cousin. The pianofortist, of course, was Mr. Christian Livingston.

Miss Keyes was garbed in a gown of white gauze draped over ivory satin, with a demi-train and a shallow edging of blond-lace round the low collar. A long strip of lace in a geometrical design ran down the center of the dress from the top of the bodice to the lace-edged hem, where it met with a pair of ivory satin sandals. Lady Keyes had wound a string of pearls six times round Daphne's throat; ear-drops and rings to match completed her jewellery. As the gown had only wisps for sleeves, her white kid gloves were elbow-length. Her hair, coiffed high in elaborate curls, was ornamented by a single ostrich plume whose soft whiteness contrasted admirably with the deep, rich darkness of her locks.

Lady Bryde inspected her critically. "She looks fine," she admitted at last to her grand-daughter; "but I've got a notion we can do some thing better for her than that ostrich feather. You wait here, gal; I've a gift for you."

Daphne murmured thanks and moved to take a seat on the long carved and gilt Confidante which dominated the drawing-room. "What are you doing, Miss?" cried the Countess sharply. Daphne held herself still immediately. "Listen to me, now. You are not to sit down—no, not if it kills you—except at dinner. Too much trouble has been taken over you today for you to go and spoil it by creasing your gown. I hope your shoes fit you." she added, a little grimly.

"They are tolerable, ma'am," said Daphne, still taken aback by the unexpected reprimand.

"Good. You must stand there until I return," the old lady instructed as she left the room, a footman opening the doors as she went. After a space of some fifteen minutes, during which the Keyes family was too nervous even to converse among themselves, she re-entered the drawing-room, a small red jewellery box in her hand. Daphne was still standing, her hands unconsciously smoothing the kid gloves over her fingers. "I see that you are obeying orders tonight," said the Countess shortly. "See that you continue. Now we've only a few minutes before the dinner guests start to arrive, so let us try to arrange this immediately. Goodbody will help you," she ended, handing the box to her dresser, who had followed her into the room.

Mrs. Goodbody opened the box and drew from it an astonishing head-dress, made of perfectly graduated pearls and hundreds of seed-pearls. "My dear ma'am!" cried Daphne, when she saw it.

"What now?" asked Lady Bryde, as if irritated. "You do not care for it?"

"Not care——! It is exquisite!" A large, tear-shaped pearl was suspended from the center of the head-dress; as Mrs. Goodbody threaded the strands of seed-pearls through her hair, Daphne saw in the pier-glass that this exotic gem was to hang in the middle of her forehead, just above the center of her brows, in a fashion which suggested the women of India. "My dear ma'am, are you certain you wish to give this to me?"

The Countess merely nodded, compressing her lips in an expression of annoyance. It was Lady Keyes who spoke, and she did so in the faraway tone of reminiscence. "My mother wore that when she made her come-out, did not she? She showed it to me. I had forgot all about it. I must thank you, Grandmamma, for giving it to Daphne. Some time her daughter will wear it too."

Lady Bryde did not answer her, but muttered something impatiently about where Lord Houghton could be. By this time the head-dress had been fastened in place, and Daphne, though she hardly dared turn her head, felt quite beautiful. Mrs. Goodbody surveyed her work, nodded as if satisfied, and quitted the drawing-room, taking the discarded ostrich feather with her. Her exit was followed presently by the entrance of Lord Houghton—who showered flatteries upon the Countess and Daphne in equal measure—and some nine or ten couples, who were to dine at Dòme House previous to the ball.

Conversation at the long dining-table turned first upon the great actor Kemble, whose intention to retire in the very near future was being bruited about by certain people who "ought to know" (as Lady Ballard, India's mother, said). "You must make a point of seeing him before he does so," Lord Houghton advised Daphne. "English boards are not likely to be trod upon by such another as he for a good long while."

The Princesse de Lieven, who sat across from Miss Keyes, interrupted him with a languid wave of the hand. "You make too much of him, Houghton," she said. "What is an actor, after all? Merely a boy who has not yet tired of dressing up in his papa's clothes, or pulling faces in his mother's glass. Actors are the drones of theatre—just as ministers are the drones of government."

"Shakespeare did not think so," objected Lord Houghton who, no longer caring to frequent Almack's, had nothing to lose in antagonizing one of its patronesses.

"Shakespeare," replied Madame de Lieven, with devastating condescension, "had a number of odd fancies." Having ornamented this opinion with a gracious and positively lethal smile, the Princesse returned her attention to her salad and declined to say any thing more until the third remove was served.

Long before that course arrived, Sir Andrew Ballard (encouraged by his wife) took notice of Daphne and addressed her for the first time. Lady Ballard, her attention drawn to Miss Keyes by the extraordinary pearl which decorated that lady's brow, had begun to toy with the notion of setting up a match between Daphne and her son William. She whispered as much to her husband while the white wine which accompanied the first remove was being poured. He responded in a terse undertone, "How much will she have?"

"I am not certain," Lady Ballard answered. "I think it must be a good deal, though."

"Find out," her husband instructed. Sir Andrew then set himself to the not very difficult task of taking a fancy to Daphne. "I suppose you like having such a fuss made about you, eh Miss?" he inquired gruffly.

"It is certainly unusual," said she.

"I should think so," he responded. "Tell me this, Miss Keyes; do you like to ride very much?"

"Yes, sir," said Daphne; "very much indeed."

"And I guess you like a trot round the Park every now and then?"

"Do you mean Hyde Park, sir?"

"Yes, of course I do."

He sounded a trifle impatient. Daphne, who was having a difficult time with a slippery forkful of peas, began to regret this seemingly pointless interrogation keenly. "I have not been there as yet," she replied, abandoning the peas.

"Well, you must go there!" said Sir Andrew. It was rather more a command than a suggestion. "How would it be if I sent young William round to take you out riding some fine morning? You've met my son William, I think?"

"O, yes. Indeed I have." A footman took her plate from before her and replaced it with another. "I should—that would be most obliging of you, sir."

"Done," said Sir Andrew, nodding an impatient, satisfied nod. "The chit's got charm," he added to his wife in a whisper. "You find out what else she's got from the Countess, eh?"

"Yes, my dear," said Lady Ballard. She was accustomed to her husband's despotic disposition, and had long since given up resenting his habit of ordering every one about, though she accepted commands from no one else. When the ladies had removed from the table to the drawing-room she set about learning Daphne's exact value in land, position, and pounds sterling.

The Princesse de Lieven overheard her there, pressing a flustered Lady Keyes for details. "Going to set her up with young William?" she inquired, yawning behind an ebony fan.

"I beg your pardon?" asked Lady Ballard, extremely annoyed with the Princesse's bluntness.

Madame de Lieven surveyed Miss Keyes, who was standing near the fire-place with her great-grandmother and smiling diligently. "She's a taking little creature," Madame observed at last. "Rustic, of course. But I see no reason why she and William should not suit."

"Really, Madame," said Lady Ballard, blinking her ice-blue eyes rapidly, "I think it is too early to be discussing such matters."

"Do you?" asked the Princesse archly. "I think your husband did not."

"My husband! Why do you——"

"I am certain every one heard, my dear," said Madame, with a smile that was part yawn. "No need to pout, Lady Ballard," she went on. "I am equally certain no one cares."

Lady Ballard was too vexed to reply. There was no need to any way, since at that moment a roar of laughter broke out at the other end of the drawing-room, and the Princesse's attention was diverted.

"Has some one said something amusing?" she called across the room.

"It is only Daphne," Lady Bryde responded. "She

wishes to know what it is about London that makes so many of the gentlemen creak."

The Princesse smiled politely. "A wit in spite of herself," she said, in a voice just loud enough to be heard.

"Sheath your claws, my dear," said Lady Bryde, not the least bit intimidated by the formidable Princess. "She is not fit adversary for you."

"No one is," the Princess observed, her smile sad and pensive. She retired behind the ebony fan to brood upon this misfortune.

The first guests for the ball began to arrive shortly before midnight. Daphne, flanked by her mother and her great-grandmother, stood at the top of the stairs to receive them. Before one o'clock she had murmured "Good-evening," "Thank you," and "So pleased to make your acquaintance" upwards of three hundred times. Her cheeks ached with smiling, her knees with courtesying, her feet with the mere effort of standing for so many hours together. The ivory satin slippers were less comfortable than she had hoped, and the lace on her collar tickled her chest. By the time the Prince of Wales arrived she scarcely noticed him, and merely bobbed a sketch of a curtsey.

"You must smile twice for this gentleman," Lady Bryde instructed her audibly. "He is the Prince Regent."

Daphne's eyes flew open and her cheeks blushed darkly. "I am so—I am so terribly sorry, your Highness," she said, executing a proper courtesy and hardly daring to look at him. The portly monarch before her did not notice any way; his eyes looked beyond her into the ball-room, as if searching for some one through the crowd.

"You seem well, Margaret," he said. "Pretty child you've got there too. Your grand-daughter, is she?"

"My great-grand-daughter," Lady Bryde corrected. "You appear in good spirits, your Highness."

"Faugh!" said he. "If you mean to 'your Highness' me, I must find some other company."

"I suppose I am expected to call you Prinny?" inquired the Countess.

"Why not?"

"I do not care for the name," she informed him. "It has always seemed to me an abominable soubriquet."

The Prince shrugged. "Tell me, how is——" he hesitated for a moment, trying to remember something. "Ah yes, how is Halston?"

"Halston?" she echoed. "Dead these fifteen years."

"Is he?" the Prince replied. His wandering attention had been caught by the appearance of a young lady of extraordinary beauty whom he had never seen before. He was no longer listening to the Countess at all. "Well, that is good. No doubt I shall find him inside some where," he said cheerfully. He smiled towards, though not quite at, her, and went off to make the acquaintance of the exquisite young woman.

"That is the man who holds the destiny of England in his hands," Lady Bryde observed blandly to Daphne. "Let it be a lesson to you."

Daphne had no idea what lesson she was meant to learn, but she smiled at her great-grandmother and turned to greet another guest. She had other things to concern herself with than the fate of the country any way. Although the dancing, of course, had not yet begun, the musicians had been playing since eleven. For some time Miss Keyes had been too much occupied with receiving her guests to pay any attention to the players, but during a lull in the arrivals just before the Regent's entrance, she had turned to observe them for the first time. Christian Livingston, unfortunately, had looked up at just that moment, and their eyes had met.

Daphne had endeavoured to smile at him, but the smile

was not returned. There had been no break in the music which flowed from the pianoforte—nor was there any disruption in the calm of Mr. Livingston's features. He had simply stared at her, apparently without recognition, and apparently without interest. In a very little while she had averted her eyes, focusing them thoughtfully upon the tips of her mother's shoes. The Prince Regent's arrival had interrupted her meditation.

The last guest whom she welcomed officially was a Mr. Frank Deever, an American whose exalted, though remote, connexions in London were responsible for his having been invited. He was a solid young man, scarcely taller than Daphne herself, but with such a brusque, forward manner that he seemed rather larger than he was in fact. His reddish face glistened with health and self-satisfaction, and the hearty smile with which he met his hostesses struck Lady Keyes as being almost exessively warm. Of course she said nothing about it to any one.

Frank Deever extracted a promise from Daphne that she would dance with him when she could, and passed on into the ball-room. The musicians, having received instructions from Lady Bryde (who preferred the old-fashioned dances of her youth), were preparing to play a minuet, the greasy violinists regarding their employer anxiously as they re-tuned their instruments. Miss Keyes was to walk the first dance with her father, naturally, after which the rest of the company was free to join them. The last thing Daphne saw before she settled her concentration to the stately steps of the dance was the luminous eyes of Christian Livingston, which had fixed upon her with a quizzical expression, and which caused her to blush extremely.

Chapter IV

It seemed to Daphne that the minuet which she danced alone with her father was rather longer than it might have been. If she had not been under inspection by the entire assembly, she would surely have been tempted to throw some glaring looks at the musicians during the trio. It was as well she could not, since she would have found her glances returned by Mr. Livingston's slightly amused gaze, and this might have distracted her, if it did not enrage her. Sir Latimer thought the dance went on a long while too, and began to perspire liberally.

When the last bars finally were struck, Latimer came to take his father's place. A contre-dance was to follow the minuet, and couples from among the guests drifted on to the floor to take their places for the first figure. Daphne, no longer feeling herself the focus of quite every one's eyes, was free to turn her attention to her feet, which hurt excessively. Since Latimer had been her constant partner when they learned to dance at Verchamp Park, they went down their two dances together easily. The two next she had promised to William Ballard, who claimed them accordingly. He was a poor dancer—worse than poor, in fact, since he was unaware of his own awkwardness and therefore caused every one round him to be awkward too, without feeling the slightest twinge of conscience.

Furthermore, he insisted on paying lengthy and elaborate compliments to Daphne as they danced, which obliged her to interrupt him when the movements of the dance required that she step away. She begged him, finally, to discontinue his flatteries.

"But they are not flatteries," he said. "Flattery implies insincerity, and I am sincere. You must forgive me, Miss Keyes; these compliments, as I should prefer to call them, rise spontaneously to my lips whenever I am near you. Your beauty——"

Daphne did not hear the end of his phrase since the music had changed and the pattern of the figure required that she turn to the gentleman on her left. She felt relieved indeed when her set with William ended.

He was replaced during the two third by Mr. Deever, who danced—as he did everything else—with inordinate energy. He was replaced in his turn by Walter, Lord Midlake, who was replaced by Lord Trugrove, who was replaced by Alexander Reade . . . and so forth, and so forth, until Daphne would sooner have consented to translate the Bible into French than to dance another dance. Happily, supper was at hand. Lord Houghton escorted her to the supper-room, where she sat down in spite of her great-grandmother's warning. She excused herself presently and went to one of the chambers which had been provided for the use of the ladies. Here she splashed cold water from a basin on her hands and cheeks, and otherwise refreshed herself. She knew she ought to return immediately to the supper-room, but her delight in finding some respite from the ball was so great that she could not prevent herself from stepping into the conservatory, which was miraculously empty of people, and enjoying her brief solitude a few more minutes.

The conservatory was a smallish apartment, but it contained a wide variety of flowers, and especially of ferns. It was behind a clump of these, on a low, unupholstered bench, that Daphne concealed herself. Marvelling at her own courage, she dared to remove her slippers and rub her feet. If the Countess, or even one of her footmen, were to discover her there she would surely be severely reprimanded. Fortunately, neither Lady Bryde nor her servants observed her. Unfortunately, Christian Livingston did.

For a little while he remained silent, watching Miss Keyes quietly over the tops of the ferns. He had chosen this moment for a recess too, leaving the violinists to play trios for the benefit of the company. The apparent unpopularity of the conservatory had drawn him, and he was as surprised to happen upon Daphne as she was, a few moments later, to see him.

"I beg your pardon," she exclaimed, unconsciously assuming that he had more right to be there than she.

"I see no reason why you ought to," he answered evenly. "I am the intruder, after all."

"O no——" she began. Then, realizing that her slippers were still upside-down upon the floor, she bent and donned them hastily. "Should you like to sit down?" she asked, springing up from the bench.

"Not if it means your standing up," he bowed.

"But it does not. That is—I do not know why I stood just now. I am sorry." She seated herself again at one end of the bench.

"Perhaps you do not like to sit next to your great-grandmother's employees," he suggested, still on his feet.

"Perhaps . . . O please, that is so silly. Do sit down; I beg you will."

"If you are quite certain——"

"I am quite certain, Mr. Livingston."

Mr. Livingston obliged her. "You recall my name, then," he remarked. "You are very clever."

"There is nothing clever in recalling the names of one's acquaintances."

"Am I to be counted among your acquaintances?" asked he, apparently amazed.

"But why not?"

"Our stations in life, Miss Keyes, are rather—disparate."

"I do not see what that is to do with it."

"Then you are not as clever as I thought."

Daphne searched for a reply but found none. In a little while Mr. Livingston spoke again. "Won't your guests be wondering where you are?" he inquired.

"O, my guests," she echoed, frowning. "No, I do not think they will notice my absence. My great-grandmother may, however."

"But this is your night," he objected.

"If it is," she murmured in a tone slightly grim, "let us hope I never have another."

There was a pause. "You really are a very curious young lady, aren't you?" Christian said at last.

"Am I? Why do you say so?"

"I imagine most girls pass the night of their come-out in an absolute swoon of rapture. Yet you seem hardly to care."

"On the contrary, I care very much. My feet ache extremely."

Mr. Livingston laughed for the first time. His laugh was low and came from deep within his chest. "I am sorry to hear it," he said, his green eyes smiling at her.

"I appreciate your condolences," she said. She began to feel at ease with him, and sat back a little on the bench. "I suppose your hands must be equally weary?"

"They are accustomed to such work."

"Is it work to you?" she asked.

He shrugged. "Music is my life, but it must also be my living. When I am at leisure to indulge my artistry, I am happy. On such an evening as this, however, it is merely my trade." In answer to her puzzled glance, he continued, "I do not particularly care for minuets and contre-dances. The need to keep the metre precise for the dancers prohibits any interpretation."

"What do you like to play?"

"O, anything else. Nocturnes, sonatas, concertos when I have the opportunity . . . even waltzes are more interesting. Lady Bryde stipulated that there was to be no waltzing tonight," he added.

"No, of course," she mused. "I understand it is still considered scandalous by some people in London. It is certainly deemed so in the country."

He looked directly at her. "Have you attempted it in spite of that?"

"Never," she cried guiltily. "O dear, that is not quite true. My brother and I—did—once. After the dancing-master had gone home. I suppose it was very bad of us."

Mr. Livingston laughed again. "Despicable," he agreed.

She hesitated a moment. "I enjoyed it excessively," she confided at last.

"Well!" he said, rather bitterly. "So the English aristocracy condescends to admit to pleasure every now and then. I had no notion."

Daphne experienced a surge of boldness. "You are very conscious of that, aren't you sir? Of rank, and position, I mean."

Mr. Livingston's eyes clouded over. "You are very naïve about it," he said. In a short time he rose and they excused themselves to one another. Daphne returned to the supper-room, and then to the ball-room, executing her duties in each place with weary obedience. When the night at last was over she learned, to her astonishment, that she was expected to have enjoyed it and to thank her great-grandmother profusely. Instructed to that effect by Lady Keyes, she mustered up a few grateful phrases and delivered them to the Countess. Happily, that lady was not in a humour to receive them.

"Never mind all that, gal," she interrupted. "You passed, any way. Madame de Lieven promised to send your family vouchers for Almack's next week. You ought to be proud of yourself."

"I am sure I made a great number of mistakes," said Daphne humbly.

"If you did they weren't crucial," said her Ladyship. "Now get to bed and stay there. I know I am ready to do so."

Daphne dropped one final courtesy and descended with her family to the coach. On the way home she fell asleep, leaning against her brother's shoulder, and dreamed of a land inhabited exclusively by hands and feet.

The vouchers for Almack's arrived on a Monday morning. Sir Latimer and Lady Keyes were in the breakfast-parlour, involved in an anxious discussion concerning when, how, and if they ought to be used when James appeared bearing a silver tray with a card upon it. This he tendered to my Lady, who accepted it and discovered that it belonged to Mr. William Ballard, Esq. She looked nervously at her husband. "He must wish to see Daphne," she said. "I shall be obliged to receive him with her, and to sit with them."

"Very well, my dear."

"But what about Almack's?" she protested.

"O, indeed. James, you may first tell Mr. Ballard that her Ladyship is in. After that, please send Mr. Clayton to me. I have business to discuss with him."

James bowed and disappeared discreetly.

"Clayton will know about Almack's," said Sir Latimer, blinking benignly at his wife. "You go and fetch Daphne."

"If you think so, dear," she said faintly, and hurried from the room.

James had shown William Ballard into the drawing-room, and it was there that Latimer happened upon him.

"Good-morning," he said jovially. "Didn't know you were here."

"I've just come," William returned. "I believe your mother has been apprised of my arrival, and that she has been kind enough not to deny me."

"You've come to wait upon my mother?" Latimer asked incredulously.

William smiled. "Frankly, I wondered if your sister would care to ride out with me."

"O, I am sure she will like to. In fact, I should like to myself. Would you mind awfully?"

Mr. Ballard had no time in which to reply, since the ladies entered at that moment and a series of greetings had to be exchanged. Latimer interrupted all of these, saying, "Daph, William here wants us to go riding with him. Should you like to?"

Daphne would actually have preferred to remain at home, but she did not know how to refuse such an invitation. She looked from her brother to Mr. Ballard. "I should be very pleased—that is, if my mother has no objections?"

"None at all," Lady Keyes reassured her. "Mr. Ballard, may I offer you some refreshments?"

"No, nothing ma'am, I thank you."

Daphne had been about to sit down upon the blue-and-white arm-chair, but her movement was checked by her brother. "Don't dawdle, Daph," he said, apparently burdened this morning with an excess of impatience. "Go and put on your riding-habit—there's a dear sister."

Coming from any one else, this sort of criticism would have crushed Miss Keyes. From her brother she accepted it with an indulgent smile. She excused herself to the company and went to her bed-chamber. Her riding-habit was a close-fitting one, and she was obliged to call upon her mother's abigail for assistance in donning the snug jacket. This done, she pulled a pair of blue kid gloves—of the same shade as the habit—on to her hands and took up her riding crop. The heels on her half-boots elevated her a full inch, so that she was nearly as tall as William himself when he rose to escort her to the door. Latimer, who had fetched his crop and changed into boots and breeches, descended to the street behind them, striking the crop cheerfully against his leg as he did so.

Young William led the way both to the Park and within it. Daphne found his guidance unnecessary and oppressive. Such a lot of "turn right's" and "turn left's," even when it was quite obvious they had no choice but to turn as he indicated! It made her nervous, and she communicated this agitation to her horse, if to no one else. When they reached a wide, empty thoroughfare in the heart of the Park, Daphne longed to gallop, or at least to canter. Mr. Ballard insisted on a dignified trot, smiling and assuring her that she really did not desire to go faster. When he was not instructing her as to what she wanted, he was pacing alongside her, a steady stream of trivialities and compliments on his lips. For a while Latimer straggled behind them, but he found this position too irksome at last and broke out into a hard gallop, hastening past them at breakneck speed. Daphne watched wistfully.

All in all she found it a most disappointing excursion. She resolved to ride out with Latimer next time, and no one else.

William left them shortly after their return to Finchley House, taking time first to inform Miss Keyes that she was the handiest rider he had ever seen—handiest female rider, that is—and to promise that he would convey her compliments to his sister. Daphne wondered silently how on earth he could have an opinion of her riding when she had done no more than to stay atop a plodding horse for an hour or two, but she smiled and bid him good-bye civilly. Lady Keyes, learning that they had come home, welcomed her children with the news that they were to go to Almack's that night—this having been the advice of Mr. Clayton. Although unusually early hours were kept at Almack's, Daphne was requested to go to her bedchamber and rest for an hour or two. "For you want to look well tonight," her mother reminded her worriedly. "It won't do to be fatigued."

Daphne obeyed, and indeed none of the family appeared to be weary when they assembled that evening in the drawing-room. Latimer was dressed, as he informed them, "bang-up to the nines." His sister, whose pretensions to modishness were somewhat less grand, looked quite attractive as well, her pale blue gown complemented by ribands of the same colour and slippers to match. Sir Latimer had sent Clayton out to purchase a better snuffbox than the one his son had objected to, and now proudly held out this trinket for all to inspect. It won approval from everyone, being made in silver and set with an ancient ivory cameo. Lady Keyes unfolded her tortoise-shell and silken fan, holding it against her dark green gown to be certain the colours agreed with one another and, satisfied, folded it up again. The Keyes family judged itself ready to set out, and consequently entered the coach directly.

They arrived at Almack's some time before eleven, and found a set of quadrilles in progress. The main saloon was crowded, and they shrank towards the walls to keep out from under the feet of the dancers. For a little while, Daphne tried to see through the mass of people to be certain of the identity of the pianofortist, but it was not really necessary: she had already recognized the distinctive style (in spite of what he said about metre) of Christian Livingston. Her endeavours to confirm this by a glance at his face were interrupted any way by India Ballard, who appeared at her side from out of the press of people. "You do look pretty," said India, tugging playfully at one of the ribands which hung from Daphne's curly locks—though not so strongly as to disarrange them.

"Thank you," she smiled; "though I think you look a good deal prettier tonight." Miss Ballard's gown was indeed gorgeous, being done in deep yellow satin and trimmed with tinsel drawn work at the hem and wrists. Yellow roses crowned her hair, and their fragrance drifted in swirls round her.

"O, as for that," said India, pulling a face, "it is my mother who did all the fussing over me. My parents wished me to appear to advantage tonight: Walter Midlake is here, and they are still hoping he will offer for me."

"Indeed? And do you think he will?"

India looked skyward, her expression at once comical and annoyed. "I am sure I have no notion. All I know is that he did not do so all last Season, nor at any time during the intervening year . . . so I see no reason to expect he will now."

"Should you like him to?" Daphne asked timidly.

Miss Ballard's gaze became harsh, and her voice followed suit. "I suppose so. Why not? At least then my parents will stop pushing me at him—and him at me, poor thing."

Daphne considered this answer. "Where is he?" she asked at last.

"There," said India, looking to a far corner of the room. "The one who has just spilled his punch, and is making such a noise laughing about it."

Daphne followed her gaze and perceived a tall, ungainly man of about thirty years of age. His ears were extraordinarily long, and his complexion sallow; other than that, he was pleasant-looking enough. She remembered, vaguely, having danced with him once at her come-out. Latimer, she noticed, was standing a few feet from him, downing a cup of punch and talking with Frank Deever.

"My dear," Daphne said finally, placing a hand on India's arm, "do you love him very much?"

"Love him?" India laughed. "Not at all. What makes you ask such a question?"

"But your parents," she returned, confused; "why do they hope he will offer for you?"

"Because," she said heavily, "he has two estates, a town-house, and five thousand pounds a year. What other reason must they have?"

"I—I do not know." Farther than this Daphne could say nothing. She did not wish to imply that she thought India's parents cruel, but that was indeed her opinion. Moreover, she could not be certain that India cared for the match as little as she appeared to. Perhaps she felt humiliated by Lord Midlake's failure to speak for her, and therefore feigned indifference. She was saved from having to elaborate upon her reply by India's turning the topic.

"Have you seen the pianofortist?" she inquired. "It is the one we met at Lady Mufftow's."

"Is it?" said Daphne, blushing at her own duplicity. "I—I was not sure."

"Do you recall his name? I cannot."

"I believe it is—" her cheeks coloured a shade more deeply, "—Mr. Livingston, is it not?"

"My dear Daphne, why are you blushing?" India demanded.

"O, it is—no reason. Perhaps it is warm in here?"

"It is not warm in here at all. Daphne, is it possible you are developing a partiality for our friend?"

"I am—O no, that is . . ." she faltered.

"I saw him at your come-out," India went on. "Did you speak to him again?"

"O no! Only for a moment, I mean. It was by chance, utterly. He is very kind, you know."

"I am certain he is," said India slowly. "Well my dear, you must try to interest yourself in some one a little more eligible—believe me. No good can come of your forming an attachment for a pianofortist."

"No, of course not," she replied, laughing nervously. "It is dreadful, the way I blush. It is merely the recollection of having met with him again—by chance, you know . . ." her voice trailed off. The music had changed by now, and Lord Midlake came over to solicit Miss Ballard's hand for the dance. Daphne observed her narrowly as she accepted, but could find no evidence for her suspicion that India's indifference to him was merely pretense. On the contrary, nothing could have been more artificial than the smile with which she greeted him, and nothing more real than the reluctance which a quiver in her voice betrayed. Miss Keyes began to feel her friend's lot a very sad one indeed.

Her own hand being claimed soon after by William Ballard, she put a period to these meditations and applied herself to the steps of the dance. As the evening wore on, she saw and spoke to several persons whom she recognized, having met them at her come-out and elsewhere.

Her mother, she observed, was deep in conversation during most of the evening with Lady Mufftow. Latimer had disappeared early to the refreshment table in the company of Mr. Frank Deever, and she saw very little of him. While she was sorry to do without her brother's attendance, she reflected that it was just as well he had taken Mr. Deever away. The American really was a difficult partner to keep up with.

The two gentlemen whom she contemplated were, though she did not know it, hanging close to the punchbowl and having a very jolly time discussing horseflesh and hunting. Latimer, turning to refill his glass, paused to inquire of his companion if he could discern the ingredients, remarking that it seemed to him that it had rather a bite to it.

"O, quite a bit of brandy in there, I should guess," Mr. Deever, Esquire, responded jocosely. His smile broadened for no apparent reason as he added, "Take care not to drink too much, now. You're liable to get drunk."

"O, I've never been intoxicated," Latimer returned carelessly; "though I've often wondered what it's like."

"Great fun," Mr. Deever assured him. "Whole world looks rosy, that's what it's like. Of course, a fellow has a hard time keeping his balance. Take care you don't overdo it—you might start talking too loudly, and then where would we be?"

"No fear of that," said Latimer, re-filling his cup and offering to do the same for Mr. Deever. "I can hold my wine well enough, I think. A little punch won't hurt me."

And as the gentlemen talked he re-filled his glass again and again. Every now and then Mr. Deever would remark that he was beginning to feel a trifle bosky himself—wasn't his friend Latimer? Smiling his broad smile, he would caution him not to drink too much. Invariably, Mr. Keyes reassured him there was no cause for concern. He continued to affirm his sobriety even as he imagined he felt just the smallest bit dizzy—then felt sure he was dizzy—then knew he was very dizzy indeed. All the while he talked about horses, and dipped liberally into the bowl.

His sister, meanwhile, went down nearly every dance, and was delighted this evening with the exercise. Her cheeks recovered the glow they had lost since her arrival in London, and her dark eyes shone. She knew she would do better not to, but she could not refrain from glancing ever and anon at Mr. Livingston, who played dance after dance with consistent skill. Several times he caught her glance, and each time he smiled—a smile which she returned easily but felt guilty about afterwards. India was right; she must really learn to govern herself more firmly. Resolutely, she would turn her eyes from him—but in a few minutes they would travel towards him again, herself unconscious that they had done so until he met her gaze and answered it. It was all very vexatious, and Daphne considered it fortunate that they had no opportunity to talk.

When Sir Latimer decided he had seen enough of Almack's and went to the refreshment-room to fetch his son, he found him in rather a remarkable state. Latimer's eyes appeared glazed; he reeled slightly while turning to meet his father, and his speech was slurred. "Frank Deever," he said, pointing at the American. "Friend. Frank—m'father."

"What's wrong with you, young man?" demanded his father. "Do you feel ill?"

"No," said his son. He pivoted around his index finger until it was pointing at the punch-bowl. "Punch," he explained.

"Has he been drinking all night?" Sir Latimer asked Mr. Deever.

"Indeed he has, sir—but there is no cause for concern.

There is nothing intoxicating in the punch, I assure you."

"That is what I thought," agreed Sir Latimer. "Lady Keyes told me nothing intoxicating at all is served at Almack's."

Young Latimer picked his head up upon hearing this, and turned to face Mr. Deever. "Tha's impossible. Tha's —ridicklish. Why, you told me yourshelf . . ."

Mr. Deever exploded in raucous laughter. "It's a joke!" he exclaimed. "A famous joke! Just wait till I tell my cousins. They'll roar!" And so saying he bowed, still chuckling, to Sir Latimer and removed himself from their vicinity.

Latimer's confusion was fast subsiding into acute embarrassment. Once the suggestion that he ought to be foxed was removed, he found he could handle himself perfectly well. He blushed to the tips of his ears. "O God," he said; "I've been making a cake of myself all night. Let's go home, Father. Please," he added.

"We are going home," said the older man. "That is precisely why I was looking for you." He took his son's arm. All the way to the door Latimer kept his eyes averted, not daring to look up for fear he should meet the mocking gaze of some of the gentlemen who had been watching— and, he was sure, laughing at—his parody of drunkenness. On the way home in the carriage he held his head in his hands and moaned about the disgrace. Daphne and his parents laughed it off, assuring him that no one, probably, had even noticed—but he was inconsolable. "That Deever," he muttered every now and then. "O! That Frank Deever."

"It *was* very bad of him," Daphne agreed.

"I am astonished his mother should have let him leave America alone!" said Lady Keyes. "I hope I have brought up my son to make better jokes than that."

But Latimer continued to moan and mutter. He shut

himself up in his bed-room as soon as possible, relieved to be alone at last. A few moment's reflection in solitude convinced him that he could never go into Society again—at least not until years had passed. But how was he to accomplish this aim? He let his candle burn late into the night, pacing up and down his room. At last a plan occurred to him: a scheme which would keep him out of Society for a good long while, and make a hero of him by the time he re-entered it. It would hurt his family at first—but that was unavoidable. His mind buzzing with schemes and preparations, he climbed into bed and extinguished the candle. In the morning he awoke before dawn and, taking very little with him, slipped out of Finchley House for ever.

Chapter V

Mid-day found Latimer somewhat uncomfortably ensconced at a table in The Angel, in the dockside town of Rotherhithe. He had found a hackney-coach at no great distance from Grosvenor Square, the jarvey asleep on the box. Instructing him rather vaguely to drive east along the Thames until directed to stop, Latimer climbed into the coach and craned his neck out the window. He kept a close watch on the River, especially after they had passed out of London, and when they reached Rotherhithe he judged that they had come far enough. Paying the jarvey, he descended into the streets and began to walk.

He strolled about all morning, through the town and by the bank of the River, spirits soaring and nostrils flaring as he breathed in the exotic scents. Most of these were unpleasant, being the smells of squalor in the town and of tar by the water, but they were all equally new to him and consequently invigourating. He dug his hands into his pockets and rambled out on to the docks, picking up the odours of spices and fragrant lumber as he went, as well as getting in the way of not a few sailors. About noon-time he began to feel hungry, and he had a double purpose when he trailed along behind a small group of sailors who were approaching The Angel. Not knowing how to secure their permission, he simply sat down at the same table as they and waited for them to take note of him.

64

He was not obliged to wait long, since his clothes, if nothing else, made him rather conspicuous. "Hallo," said one of the seafarers to his companions, "I do believe we got a new face at this table—and I do believe it's a swell." The man who spoke thus was about thirty-five years of age. Swarthy like his fellows, his scant teeth and lop-sided nose testified to years of hard living. He grinned enormously as he jerked a thumb at Latimer. Lady Keyes would have had no trouble in identifying him as an unsavoury character, but her son rather liked him.

One of his colleagues, a wiry man with rapidly thinning blond hair, agreed with him. "It looks like a swell—aye, bloody like one."

"What will we do with it, lads?" asked the first.

"Well, we might knock it about a bit," another suggested.

"What?" cried the first. "Wi'out asking it its name? Shame on you for a brute wi' no manners!"

"He's right, Tom," said the blond one. "That would be bloody impolite, knocking it about without asking its name."

The one called Tom shrugged. "Then let's ask it," he said.

At this point Latimer spoke up. "My name's Latimer— Latimer K——" he paused a moment—"Cross," he ended. "Pleased to make your acquaintances."

"Pleased to make yours," said Tom, sneering.

"Your manners, Tom; your manners!" chided the first sailor. "You want to tell him your name as well. Cross, m'boy, this here's Tom, and this other one is Alf. You can call me Plunk, since everybody does, and nobody knows my right name except my dear old mother." He winked and grinned again.

Latimer extended his hand to shake those of his new friends. No one took it.

"Do we knock him about now, Plunk?" asked Alf.

"O, I don't know as we will do that," he replied. "I'm starting to take quite a shine to the lad, almost like he's my own son. Just what might a regular swell like yourself be doing down here, Mr. Cross?"

"I've come to join the Navy," said Latimer, as the serving woman came to the table and ladled out bowls of greasy stew for each of them.

"O, the Navy is it?" Plunk asked, taking a moment for a wide look and a wink at his companions. "Going to be a Admiral, I guess?"

"Well, maybe," Latimer answered with an humble smile.

"If you mean to be a Admiral, Mr. Cross, I think you'd best ask your dad to purchase that title for you. Save time, see what I mean?"

"I don't have a family," said Latimer, his cheeks flushing.

"O, don't you now? And since when is that?"

"Since—a long time ago."

"All on your own, is it?"

"Yes," Latimer agreed. "All on my own."

"Well, I declare," said Plunk. "Got any money?"

"Only a little," Latimer replied nervously. "I'll pay for this, though," he added, indicating the meal on the table.

"You will, eh? No, we wouldn't think of letting you do that, now would we boys?"

"I would," said Tom.

"So would I," Alf seconded.

For the first time, Plunk's grin vanished and he glared at his friends. Then he beckoned to them and they leaned over, their three heads whispering together. In a short time they drew apart again and Plunk once more addressed Latimer.

"My mates and I have took a real liking to you, my boy," he said. "Here's what we're going to do. Now we ain't in the Navy, as you may have guessed by these—" he indicated his soiled clothing by plucking at the shoulders of his own shirt, "and we don't suppose plain sailing would be good enough for you, since you're a-going to be a Admiral."

Latimer agreed that it wouldn't.

"Howsoever," Plunk continued, "you'll need to have your sea-legs when you go into the Navy, so here's what we propose. You come down to the ship with us today and walk about a bit. She ain't too big a ship, but at least you can learn port from starboard on her. I'll fix things wi' the Captain so he won't mind your coming." He winked again at his colleagues. "Then, when you got your sea-legs on good and tight, we'll take you to a place we know of in London where you can meet some real Navy chaps—maybe even some officers. Then tomorrow you can join up with them, and by next week you can be a Admiral. What do you say?"

Latimer knew perfectly well his ambitions were being laughed at, but the sailors' scheme sounded like a good one to him any way. He agreed therefore, thanked them, argued over who was to settle with the inn-keeper, and went off with them to spend the day at the docks. The fact that they would not allow him to pay for the meal at The Angel re-assured him of their good intentions, and it seemed to him, as he applied himself to learning nautical vocabulary, that his plans were proceeding very well indeed.

He was pleased to find that he did not feel the least bit queasy, though as the day wore on he became increasingly aware that the sun was burning his forehead and the ropes were burning his hands. A trip to The Angel for supper and ale refreshed him somewhat, and when the last round had been ordered and drunk, he sat back in his chair like the others and listened avidly to their conversation.

"I say we go to McGinty's," Alf suggested, wiping his mouth with the back of his hand.

"The Quarter-Deck has got more tables," Tom disagreed.

"I still say McGinty's."

"Settle it, Plunk," Tom requested.

"Me, mates?" said Plunk, as if astonished at being applied to. "Well, if it was left to me, I'd say we ought to call at Mrs. Stott's establishment."

"Stott's?" Tom objected. He lowered his voice and spoke earnestly to Plunk. "I seen Quality in there, two or three times now. I know the stakes are higher, but . . ." his voice faded and he cast a meaningful glance at Latimer.

"Now, now," said Plunk heartily, "you've no objections to going to a place where you might meet a friend or two, have you my boy?" he asked Latimer. "Seeing as how you're all on your own, and so forth."

"N-No," said Latimer, adding resolutely, "of course not." It had become clear to him that his new friends meant to visit a gaming-house tonight; he did not think it too likely that any of his London acquaintance would frequent such places. Any way, having convinced the sailors of his independence, he could not cry craven now.

"There, you see?" Plunk was saying to Tom. "Cross here has no objections. Now you just quit your worritting and mind your manners like I told you."

Tom nodded but spat vehemently, as if to signify that he was under no obligation to submit to Plunk's bullying.

A waggoner who sat at a table nearby and was on the road to London agreed to take them there for a small fee. The sailors sprang in with him and descended some hours later in a part of the town which Latimer had never seen.

The narrow streets were laid out crookedly and no lamp illuminated them. Raucous laughter issued from several of the doors they passed, and a thin, faraway wail rose up and pierced the air again and again. Refuse lined the pavement and in a grey, huddled mass wedged against a door-way, Latimer discerned the outlines of a woman—a beggar with no refuge from the thickening night. When they had walked about a mile through this maze, Plunk knocked at a door with fresh black paint on it and whispered a few words to the woman who peeped out. When she had stepped back and permitted them to enter, Latimer had his first look at a gaming-hell.

The house was much better furnished than its exterior promised, and though the colours were gaudy and the upholstery cheap, it had a busy, prosperous air. The men removed their coats, handing them to the young woman who had admitted them, and proceeded directly up the narrow wooden stairs. Alf pinched the girl on her cheek and called her "darling," but she did not respond. The second story of the house was divided into two large rooms, one devoted to Hazard, the other to Faro and similar games at cards. It was to the first of these that Plunk led them.

The voices of the players were so loud as to obscure the rattle of dice altogether. Clouds of smoke hovered just under the low ceiling, and the unpleasant odour of mutton-fat tapers pervaded the atmosphere. Most of the gentlemen present appeared to be sailors; all of them, certainly, came from a class of which Latimer had had very little experience. If there were any "Navy chaps" among them, as Plunk had promised, they were out of uniform. Though he began to feel, unwillingly, that there might be something sinister in his situation, at least Latimer had no fears of meeting anyone he knew. Alf's idea of Quality and his own apparently did not coincide.

Mrs. Stott, a florid woman in a gown of slippery purple stuff, greeted the newcomers at the top of the stair-case. "English Hazard or French?" she asked, when Plunk had made an elaborate, insolent bow and introduced Latimer to the proprietess.

"English, m'dear," he replied. "None of your foreign nonsense for us."

Mrs. Stott's smile only partially concealed her disappointment, for she preferred her clientele to bet against the bank, rather than against each other. Still, Plunk and his crew were liberal with their blunt—when they had any—and she could not afford to appear ungracious. "Got yourself a fat chicken, eh?" she whispered to Plunk as he passed inside.

Plunk merely smiled and repeated his satirical bow to the lady. He then turned his attention to Latimer, and did not take it from him until the end of the evening.

Mr. Keyes had never played at Hazard, either English or otherwise, and to expect him to distinguish himself at it on this first occasion—even under normal circumstances—would be to expect a great deal. His ineptitude as a beginner was exacerbated by the fact that these, of course, were not normal circumstances at all. His three gaming companions were, in fact, firmly united in their intention to make him lose as much as possible, and in this they succeeded very well. They forced upon him stakes much higher than any they would set among themselves; they plied him with quantities of nauseating gin, obligingly supplied by the cooperative Mrs. Stott; and whenever he seemed about to cry off, they mocked him severely and assured him of their willingness to accept his signature in lieu of hard cash. By the end of the evening—which seemed to Latimer to go on for ever—Plunk held notes from him which bound him to the payment of a sum exceeding three hundred pounds. At that point the sailors agreed that, in their words, Latimer had been "thoroughly plucked," and was ready to be let go.

He emerged reeling onto the foggy street. His companions had given up all pretense of camaraderie and did not offer to find a bed for him for the night. Instead, they insisted that he lead them to his parents' door—boxing his ears when he protested that he had none—so that they would know where to find him if he failed to pay his debts. Tom was for making him wake his father and securing a bank draught immediately, but Plunk judged this course too dangerous and merely cautioned their prey to come up with the money before next week. On these words they left him, and Latimer, feeling he had reached the extreme depth of degradation and folly, knocked upon the door. All were awake within, of course, for his disappearance had been the cause of the liveliest alarm, and James opened immediately. Latimer crawled inside in an agony of defeat.

The Prodigal Son himself did not receive a more compassionate welcome that did Latimer from his family. Lady Keyes wept, Daphne wept—even Sir Latimer might have been observed wiping a tear of relief from the corner of his eye. They had spent their day sunk in the most anxious conjecture, and nothing but Mr. Clayton's earnest counsel prevented them from sending to Bow Street and launching an investigation that very day. Sir Latimer had meant to do so at dawn any way.

Though the hour was considerably advanced, and everyone exhausted, Lady Keyes insisted on a complete account of her son's most eventful day. Stalwartly overcoming his natural reluctance, Latimer made a clean breast of it, reclining gratefully on the carved and gilt settee and sipping the cordial his mother had pressed upon him. When he mentioned the sum he had signed away, there was a general outcry.

"Above three hundred!" Daphne gasped. "O Latimer!"

"But I did not sign for it in my right name," he protested. "I do not believe I can be held accountable, under the circumstances." He turned towards the mantelpiece, by which Mr. Clayton was standing. "Must I pay it, Clayton? I signed the notes 'Latimer Cross.' "

Mr. Clayton shut his protruding eyes and considered, holding a finger up to indicate that he would speak in a moment. "I do not think so," he said at last. "However, the scoundrels might try to press charges—and in that case, a scandal would inevitably follow. I believe my Lady Bryde would be most unhappy if that were to happen."

"O indeed!" cried Lady Keyes, distressed at the mere thought of her grandmother's response to such an eventuality. "We must—perhaps we ought to pay them if that is our alternative." She looked imploringly at her husband, who harrumphed loudly and looked in turn at Clayton.

"I believe our best course," that gentleman continued slowly, "will be to settle with each of them for some reduced figure, and let it go at that. Their treatment of Master Latimer—who is, after all, still in his minority—was undoubtedly unlawful . . . but again, there is the problem of scandal." He paused.

"God will punish them," Lady Keyes assured him, dismayed at this fresh mention of scandals.

"Yes, of course my Lady," said Clayton. "And resting in that knowledge, we can be certain that in giving each of them, say, twenty pounds, we will be acting rightly."

"Still," said Lady Keyes, her conscience unsettled, "it hardly seems correct to reward the ruffians."

"Do you think they may yet be unsatisfied, and return to—to knock Latimer about?" asked Daphne, her dark gaze troubled.

"I am sure they will recognize that they are being treated better than they deserve to be," Mr. Clayton assured her, adding for Lady Keyes' benefit, "though not so well as to encourage them to pursue a life of crime."

The family continued to discuss the incident, and to solicit details from Latimer, for another half-hour. Then their weariness overwhelmed them and they went to bed, Lady Keyes making sure to tuck her son in securely, and exacting a promise from him that he would never attempt such a foolish scheme again. The promise was easily and sincerely given.

The following morning Lady Bryde lay abed at Dome House and sipped her morning chocolate, as she did every morning. The Keyes', quite naturally, had sent James round to her house on the previous afternoon to see if Latimer might be with his great-grandmother. Thus she had been alerted to the fact that he had disappeared, and her first plan this morning was to call at Finchley House to learn if he had been found. This project she speedily put into execution, not from any pressing desire to know, but out of a sense of duty. James opened to her and summoned Latimer to her presence in the drawing-room.

"Sit down, Latimer," she directed him, indicating a chair opposite to her own. "I will ask you several questions. Now, did you leave of your own accord?"

"Yes," he confessed.

"Did you return of your own accord?"

"No . . . not precisely."

"Any officer of the law drag you back?"

"No," he said, a small smile curling the corners of his lips, though he tried to prevent it.

"Ruffians, then?" she queried.

"Yes, ma'am."

"Did any of the *ton* see you?" she asked sharply.

"No one."

"You are certain, Latimer?"

"Quite certain, ma'am."

She sighed relief. "How much did it cost, boy?"

"About sixty pounds," he said guiltily. "It might have been more."

"It might have been much more," she agreed. She leaned back into the cushioned chair and closed her eyes. For the first time in his life, Latimer saw his great-grandmother look tired. Lady Bryde opened her eyes after a minute or two and said, "That is all. You may go."

"I am terribly sorry," he said, rising.

She waved an impatient hand. "Go, go," she said. When he had obeyed she leaned back again and shut her eyes once more. "I am old," she murmured to herself. Then she rose, let herself out of the drawing-room, and quitted Finchley House. At home again, she went to her study, scribbled a note, and summoned Hastings.

"Have this taken to Lord Houghton," she told him, handing him the note.

The butler inclined his neat, silvering head.

"And Hastings—" she added. "No, never mind. Have Goodbody bring a book to me. It does not signify which one."

The butler bowed again and disappeared.

When Lord Houghton arrived—for the note contained a request that he wait upon her directly—the Countess was seated on the red plush chair in the drawing-room of Dome House, leafing through a well-thumbed volume of Dryden. She set the book down gladly and extended a hand to her old friend.

"Anthony," she said, after he had kissed her hand, "you will not be astonished to hear, I trust, that my great-grandson has got himself into a scrape."

"Not at all," he smiled.

"No, nor was I. Neither will you be astonished to learn that he has somehow got out of it again."

Lord Houghton bowed slightly before seating himself, to indicate his agreement.

"Daphne is bound to disgrace herself as well," she said.

"I see no reason to believe——"

"No," she interrupted him. "It is quite inevitable. It is the business of youth to get into scrapes, and the business of maturity to get them out again."

"As you say," my Lord conceded, still smiling.

"But Anthony, my dear, does it never occur to you that we are growing, perhaps, too old to bother about such things?"

"Never, my love," he said. "Nothing ever occurs to me which has not occurred to you first, and I believe you have never mentioned this topic before."

Lady Bryde lifted a single eyebrow in an expression at once weary and amused. "You are gallant, my dear; always gallant."

"Gallantry is the only proper answer to charm—unless one is a wit, of course, which I have never been."

"No," she agreed, "indeed you have not. But Anthony—you are not angry with me for concurring with you, are you?" she broke off.

"Not at all. I was about to be, but I have thought better of it."

The Countess smiled for the first time. "I am considering going abroad—for an extended period," she informed him.

"London will miss you sadly," he said.

As if she had not heard him, she continued. "I should like to see some exotic lands, as they are called. Not merely the Continent this time: Europe is simply England all over again, but with longer titles—which only makes them more difficult to remember and to pronounce. No, I should like to travel to the Orient, I think, or perhaps to Africa. I am told there are deserts in Africa, and I should like to see one."

"If you long to see a desert, Margaret, I understand that London is a desert during December. Perhaps you might simply stop at Dome House over Christmas."

She smiled again but shook her head. "It will not answer, Anthony. I have my heart set on a long voyage to a far-off land, and as soon as Daphne's marriage is settled, that is exactly what I shall undertake."

"Daphne's marriage is sure to be announced this season," said Houghton. "She is undeniably charming. I am sorry indeed to hear I will lack your companionship so soon."

"But my dear Anthony, that is precisely why I sent for you. If I am going to travel to far-flung places, and see exotic things, I shall be needing an escort." She paused as if expecting an answer, but none came. "Anthony, I am asking you if you would care to join me."

"Go to Africa!" he exclaimed. "O, my dear Margaret, I do not think it would suit me at all. Any way, my presence would hardly lend propriety to your entourage; quite the contrary, in fact."

"But I do not wish to have an entourage, don't you see?" she cried. "I have been surrounded and surrounded all my life. I have had enough of Society, and enough of servants."

"Then you mean to travel with me alone?" he protested. "My dear Margaret, you must surely have gone mad. There is nothing at all proper in that—O no, nothing, at all."

"Anthony," said the Countess impatiently, laying a

frail hand upon his sleeve, "I am asking you to marry me."

For a moment, Lord Houghton could find no words. When at last he did, he spluttered. "Marry . . . at this advanced—O dear, Margaret . . . What I mean to say is, Africa, after all. But my dear! It is quite—that is, you are very good . . . but still!"

Lady Bryde listened impassively to this monologue. "I did not think you would wish to do it," she said. "Never mind."

"Well of course, any thing at all for you, my dearest rose . . . but Africa! Well that is rather too much!"

"Exactly, exactly." She patted his sleeve consolingly. "I beg you will forget I suggested it at all," she said. "I am not at a loss quite yet any way."

"Not at a loss?" he echoed, slightly calmer.

The Countess' smile became mysterious as she said, "No; I have another scheme . . . less desirable of course, but just as pleasant."

"And what is that?"

Her faded eyes were dreamy. "I cannot tell you yet; not even you, my dear. You shall see soon enough." Her expression sharpened as she added, "They shall all see. But I have made you uncomfortable, my dear," she went on. "I did not mean to. Let me give you some Madeira, shall I?"

Lord Houghton accepted, Hastings was rung for, and the refreshments were brought. When he had recovered himself some what, he began to press her, gently, to reveal her scheme, but she was adamant and would only smile. In a little while he departed and she once again took up her Dryden, leafing though it idly and smiling to herself now and then, a visionary gleam in her heavy-lidded eyes.

Chapter VI

The Season progressed, as Seasons will, the days lengthening imperceptibly as spring broadened towards summer, the costumes of the *ton* growing less substantial as its gossip grew more so, since each evening provided new opportunities for intrigue and scandal. Lady Hargreave was rumoured to have taken a lover; Lady Margold was reputed to have abandoned hers; and so on. The gentlemen strove to commit ever greater follies as they challenged one another to races, contests, and duels, gambling sums upon these which were so extravagant as to be positively bizarre. Very little of this extraordinary way of life penetrated to the Keyes family, for they followed scrupulously the precepts which Lady Bryde had set down for them and these shielded them indeed from the greater irregularities of the aristocracy. Exactly as she had predicted, in fact, they had made very little mark upon London, and were scarcely discussed at all. They went on, consequently, quite comfortably.

Christian Livingston, that remarkable pianofortist, was the talk of London this Season. No self-respecting hostess omitted to engage his services for her dancing-soirée or ball; if Mr. Livingston were unavailable, she simply changed her scheme and held a rout or card-party instead. It was generally discovered some time during May that Mr. Livingston composed as well as played, and from that time on all sorts of musical afternoons were planned and attended. There seemed no end to his popularity, and hardly a soul in London dared to deny his genius.

Daphne, of course, saw him every where. It was impossible not to, since the *ton* had made a pet of him. They smiled at one another always; on several occasions they had opportunity to speak, which they did civilly and shortly; but it was not until early June, at the Viscountess Kirkwald's modest soirée, that their acquaintanceship began to take on the cast of what might be called a liaison.

Christian had been permitted, during the early part of the evening, to play what he would. Some twenty couples sat quietly in the Viscountess' drawing-room, or stood speaking in low voices among themselves, during this performance—not a few of them finding his much-praised compositions perplexingly dissonant, and secretly hoping it would soon be over. It was, of course, and an interlude followed during which a light collation was served in the dining-room. When this repast had ended there was to be dancing. Daphne had come escorted by Latimer only, for though he was yet unwilling to go into public, their mother had succumbed to an headache—which was apparently contagious, since their father caught it too. She found Mr. Livingston's playing enchanting, as she always did, and forgot to go in to supper. On most evenings, William Ballard—whose attentions had become excruciatingly assiduous—would have been at her side to prevent her forgetting; but the Ballards had gone to the theatre tonight, since Lady Ballard had been feuding with the Viscountess Kirkwald for years. Daphne had been invited to make up one of their party, but she had declined.

Now she sat, quite lost in reverie as the themes of the last sonata echoed in her mind, in the far corner of a small mahogany Confidante which stood at one end of the drawing-room. The fact was, that someone had indeed invited her in to supper—Lord Midlake, as it happened—but she had not heard him and he had gone away, thinking confusedly that she meant it for a slight. The rest of the assembly had gone away too, and she remained in the drawing-room quite alone—except, that is, for the celebrated pianofortist.

He joined her, sitting not six inches away on the other side of the low arm-rest. Her countenance being averted and further concealed by a gloved hand held to one temple, she did not notice him even then. After a few moments he broke in upon her thoughts, saying in a low tone, "Day-dreaming, Miss Keyes?"

She looked up, considerably startled. "I beg your—O dear, is every one gone?" She looked about in confusion.

"Perhaps Miss Keyes did not sleep well last night, and is nodding now?"

Daphne faced him directly, and for the first time in her life there was an edge in her voice as she spoke. "Perhaps Miss Keyes enjoys your music, and forgot to behave as she ought."

"You sound angry," he observed.

"I am tired of having to prove to you, each time we meet, that I am not the folly-drunken fribble you insist upon taking me for." Aware, suddenly, of the tone she had used, she added stiffly, "I am sorry."

"It is I who ought to be sorry," he said. "You are correct." Impulsively, he took her hand—the ungloved one—and kissed it. His blond hair brushed her wrist, and tickled it.

"Let us forgive one another," Daphne said, with a small smile. Christian said nothing; he was looking into her eyes with the intense unself-consciousness of sudden discovery. Daphne looked back steadily into his green ones. Forgetting every faculty of mind but intuition, she tilted her head slowly backwards and raised her lips towards his. He met her with equal passion.

Her gloved hand caught at his slender wrist as they drew away from one another. She started to excuse herself but found she did not wish to say any thing. Rising, her fingers still clasped round his wrist, she bent her head and kissed his hand as he had hers. Then she released it and left the room.

She begged Latimer to take her home at once. He, being still acutely uncomfortable in society, raised no objections. When they reached Finchley House, Daphne kissed him good-night and went to bed directly.

In the morning she had an engagement with India Ballard. They were to purchase some books at Hatchard's, and Daphne needed a pair of sandals since the weather had got so warm. They were driven there in the equipage India's parents had given her on the occasion of her seventeenth birthday; a taciturn footman escorted them and followed them in and out of the shops. Lady Keyes, her headache much improved, had requested that Daphne buy her some green silken thread, for her embroidery.

The two young women talked of sandals, of poetry, of theatrical performances, and—during the drive home—of Walter Midlake. He had still said nothing, either to India or to her father, about marriage. "I *am* sorry," said Daphne, with as much conviction as she could summon up.

"Really, my dear," India replied laughing, "if you could see the way he pulls at his ears and chews his lips when he is trying to make a decision, you would not be sorry at all. Imagine having a baby with ears like that! Why, it would be impossible to love it."

"Of course," said Daphne, patting her friend's hand; "but I know it must be difficult for you, when your parents have such hopes."

"Hopes!" cried India, her voice becoming harsh again.

"They've more than hopes by now, my dear. Now they've got an elaborate scheme—all to do with a house-party this summer, at Carwaith Abbey you know, and William's coming into his majority, and goodness knows what. They seem to think that if they can but isolate my Lord from his friends he will come up to the scratch. O, and that reminds me: was Mr. Livingston at the Viscountess' party last night?"

Daphne's dismay at being asked this question was such that she forgot to inquire why the one thing had reminded Miss Ballard of the other. Her cheeks drained instantly of colour and she murmured a barely audible, "Yes."

" 'Why so pale and wan, fond lover?' " she quoted; " 'Prithee, why so pale?' O, I do apologise . . . that is Suckling, and I ought not to be quoting him when you look so ill. But my dear Daphne, what is the matter?"

" 'Between who?' " Daphne countered, hoping by parroting Hamlet to side-track her inquisitor into a battle of quotations.

"Between you and Mr. Livingston, I begin to think," said India, ignoring Miss Keyes' tempting rejoinder.

"Nothing," she whispered, her colour returning in a rush.

"If it is nothing, my dear friend, then tell me why your cheeks go from white to red so regularly. You look like a barber's pole."

Daphne endeavoured to smile and did not succeed too well.

"You are in love with him?" India pursued.

"I kissed him," she confessed.

"O," said Miss Ballard. Then, "Well, that is a relief. You merely wish to take him for a lover."

"What do you mean?" asked Daphne urgently.

"Simply that if you were in love with him you might

have been in danger—for hearts do get broke, you know. As it is . . . you have simply to wait until you marry."

"Until I marry whom?"

"Why, whomever! How should I know? Whoever it is, he is not likely to mind what you do with Mr. Livingston once he has been satisfied you were a maid when you married."

If India had felt less sympathy for her friend she would have laughed outright, so comical was the expression on Daphne's face. "Are you—quite serious?" she asked at last.

"My dear, I have never been more so. That is the way of these things; it is silly to expect otherwise. You did not—you do not hope to marry Mr. Livingston?" she exclaimed, shocked for the first time since their conversation had begun.

"No," said Daphne truthfully; "I have been too astonished at my own behaviour to think of him at all."

"You feel ashamed of yourself?"

"No," Daphne said again, this time in a whisper. "That is the terrible part. I do not feel ashamed at all."

The carriage had rolled to a stop in front of Finchley House. "You have got yourself into a muddle," said Miss Ballard, squeezing Daphne's hand. "Promise me you will do nothing about it until we've spoken again. I must run now or I would come in with you . . . Promise, will you?"

"I promise," said Daphne—but in the event it was impossible for her to keep her vow. She did not see India until next day, and she saw Mr. Livingston that night.

He was playing at a ball Lord and Lady Frane were giving to celebrate the betrothal of their daughter. Daphne suspected he would be there, since he seemed to be every where there was music, and she would have liked to cry off—but Dorothea Frane had been quite kind to her on several occasions, and it seemed a most shabby thing to do. Besides, she was to marry Charles Stickney, and Latimer liked Stickney and wanted his sister to come. She went, therefore, wearing an unremarkable gown and resolved upon remaining excessively inconspicuous if the pianofortist was indeed there.

Naturally, he was; and almost as naturally, Daphne's laudable intention to remain invisible failed. Christian discerned her dark, glossy curls as soon as she entered the ball-room. The moment she left it—this time to breathe some cooler air in the walled garden below the ball-room—he accelerated the piece he was playing and brought it to a rapid close. The dancers quite exhausted themselves trying to keep up with him and wondered, as they saw him stride across the room, where on earth he was going. Happily, no one was curious enough to follow.

Lord Frane had not been following the programme his wife had set up for the evening, and he took this interval to be the one alloted for the delivery of his speech. He rose, therefore, called for every one's attention, and prosed on at length in a congratulatory mode about brides, grooms, and children. In the deserted garden below, Christian Livingston caught up with Daphne.

"Miss Keyes," he began.

She turned and gave an involuntary gasp. "Mr. Livingston."

"You left last night without saying good-bye," he chided.

"You knew I meant it."

"I wished you had not left at all."

"Mr. Livingston, I wish you had not followed me down here."

"You are sorry to see me?" he asked.

"Yes."

"In that case," he said, bowing, "my most profound apologies." He turned and began to walk away.

"Christian!" she said, reaching out instinctively for his arm. He turned, hesitating, and looked down at her. "Do not go," she managed to say finally. "Please."

"You seem not to know what you want," he remarked.

"Indeed," she said, in a small voice; "I do not."

She looked up into his face and remembered, suddenly, how his hair had felt when it brushed her wrist. Acting too quickly even to know what she did, she reached up a hand and buried it in that silken blond mass. Somehow, her other arm circled his waist, and his closed round her. They kissed one another wordlessly, feeling at once astonished to find each other and yet easily familiar. Christian had just finished dropping kisses on her eyelids, and was about to do the same to her nose, when he drew away from her a little.

"My dear Miss Keyes," he said, smiling slightly, "do you realize I do not know your given name?"

She laughed as she told him, but her amusement soon turned to dismay. "O my dear," she said. "This is awful."

"But it means nothing," he objected, not understanding her. "I know it now: you are Daphne. A very pretty name. I did not wish to make inquiries, you know; it would have been indiscreet."

"But that is exactly what I mean!" she cried. "Why should it be indiscreet for you to know my name? It is wrong—all so very wrong."

"It is indiscreet, Miss Daphne Keyes, because we are so very far apart in the eyes of the world. I know you think I make too much of this, but I assure you: in the opinion of England, there can be no—no friendship between us without disgrace for you." They held each other loosely now, and Daphne pushed her curls back with an impatient hand.

"Then what are we to do?" she demanded.

"Precisely what we are doing now. Tryst with one another, steal time . . . it will be easier when you are married," he added.

"When I am married!" Daphne echoed. "Then you desire me to marry too?"

"Of course you must marry." Daphne dropped her hands to her sides, stepped back a little and stared at him. "I know what you are thinking," Christian went on, "and you must believe me: if there were any possibility of my marrying you, I should never suggest a clandestine arrangement. But there is not."

"And that is all there is to say to it? We cannot marry, plain and simple—so we must have—so we must see one another in secret? Is that the whole of your opinion?"

"My dear Daphne, it is either secretly or not at all. If you are considering elopement, I must beg you to think again. My career is fine at present, but next Season a new phenomenon will come along and my name will mean nothing. Besides, not all the comfort in the world could compensate for the shame and disgrace you would surely be made to suffer. I would not do it to you."

"You would not elope with me?"

"No, I would not."

For a horrible moment Daphne felt she would bury her head in her hands and cry. Then she mastered herself and, schooling her features to calm, drew herself up so she stood very straight. In a steady voice she said, "I must think about this."

"Yes, my love," he answered, reaching for her hands. She drew them away from him.

"Good-night," she said, and walked hastily back through the still evening into the house. Lord Frane had just finished his speech, and felicitations were being liberally bestowed. Daphne entered the ball-room and worked her way through the crowd to Dorothea. "I wish you very happy," she said warmly, embracing her with a smile. In a short time Mr. Livingston returned to his instrument, and the dancing began again.

India called at two o'clock on the following day, and Daphne, after drawing her up to her bed-chamber so they could have a tête-à-tête, confessed every detail of her interview with Christian. She suppressed only the quality of her emotions, and with what strength they were aroused. When she had done India smiled at her and took up her hand.

"You see, my dear; I was right. I am glad he knows it, since you do not."

"But is this all there can be between us?" Daphne asked, still incredulous.

"It is a good deal more than there is between myself and any man. What more do you desire?" India returned.

"But can I trust him at all? Would an honourable man consent to such a—a liaison? Surely, he ought to chuse not to see me at all, when this is the alternative."

"Daphne, I have run out of ways to tell you," cried Miss Ballard, with mock exasperation. "Whom will you believe? Any man would consent to see you secretly, if he could not do so openly—if he wanted to see you enough, that is. It is a measure of his love for you, in fact, for you must know he runs risks in doing it."

"But what of his respect for me? For himself?"

"Love excludes the possibility of respect—or rather, it makes it irrelevant."

"It does not for me," said Daphne stubbornly. In a short while she grew ashamed of this perverse announcement and remembered to thank her friend. "How did you become so wise?" she asked wonderingly; "how do you know so many things?"

India's eyes became curiously expressionless. "I do not

know myself," she said slowly. "I seem always to have known them."

They were silent for a long time, sitting with hands linked on Daphne's bed.

"What will you do?" India asked at last.

"I have not decided."

"I think my brother means to offer for you," Miss Ballard said soberly.

"I know," she responded. "I know."

When India had gone, Daphne remained in her bedchamber. She continued to sit there for several hours, her legs folded up and hugged tightly to her chest, her chin upon her knees, her dark eyes large and wondering. When she rose at last and joined her family at dinner, she had made a decision. She would not speak to Christian Livingston again; if forced to do so, she would give him the cut direct. As much as possible, she would cease to think of him. It had occurred to her at one point to speak to Lady Bryde about it, to apply for her permission to make a match with the pianofortist. Some instinct told her, however, that her great-grandmother's advice would be exactly the same as India Ballard's. A similar instinct told her that to approach her parents with the problem would only cause them confusion—from which they would turn naturally to Lady Bryde. She felt she had grown three years older in as many hours, and begged to be excused from the excursion her family planned to make to Vauxhall that evening. When questioned by her mother, she explained that she was exhausted. Lady Keyes put a hand to her daughter's forehead and concluded that she had a fever—slight, but discernible. Daphne was put to bed and told to go to sleep—a command which she obeyed with the greatest willingness.

When she awoke she was still feverish. She discovered to her great surprise that she had slept twelve hours, and that a physician had been summoned. Mr. Whiting had been recommended to her by Lady Ballard, her mother told Daphne, but he would not be able to come round until late that afternoon. Until then Daphne was to lie quietly, and to try to take some tea.

"You look terribly tired, Mamma," she said, sitting up against the pillows. "Are you well yourself?"

"Quite well, my dear," said Lady Keyes. She indicated the cup which Daphne held in her hand. "Try to drink it."

"You haven't been sitting up all night with me?" Daphne cried.

"Your tea, Daphne," Lady Keyes replied.

"O, Mamma, you have! You must go to bed immediately; I won't have it. I feel perfectly fit."

"Well you look dreadful," Lady Keyes said frankly, and this was true. Daphne's cheeks were flaming with fever, and her eyes were glazed and unnaturally bright. "I will go to bed when you have drunk your tea."

"Do not wait, please," said she.

Lady Keyes smiled wanly and pointed at the cup.

"I can't drink it," Daphne confessed at last. "The very odour of it is making me feel ill."

"O my dear," said Lady Keyes. She took the cup and set it down on the night-stand. Then she threw her arms round her daughter. "Forgive me," she said, releasing her after a moment; "I must be making it worse for you."

"But no, Mamma! You are a great comfort."

Lady Keyes' eyes became as glassy as her daughter's, then welled over into tears. "I am sorry," she sniffed, dabbing at her eyes with a cambric handkerchief. "I know I oughtn't to worry."

"Indeed you ought not, Mamma. If you were not sleepy you would not be so foolish." As she mentioned sleep, she realized all at once how tired she was. Nothing seemed sweeter than to lean back . . . to close her eyes . . . to drift into delicious slumber. She did not wake again until the doctor came.

Mr. Whiting examined his patient at dusk. When he had finished, he bowed to Lady Keyes (who still had not slept) and requested that she follow him out of the bed-chamber. Closing the bedroom door softly, he spoke to her in a low tone.

"Is your daughter of a nervous disposition?" he inquired.

"Not at all," said her Ladyship.

"Is she frequently agitated? Subject to hysteria, or to fainting?"

"Never. Daphne has always been perfectly healthy."

"Not prone to melancholy? Fits of moroseness, ill-humor?"

"Not in the least," she replied.

Mr. Whiting tried another tack. "Has any thing occurred in the past few days to put her out of frame?"

"Well, nothing that I know of. Mr. Whiting, what is wrong with my daughter?" she demanded.

"So far as I can determine, Lady Keyes, there is nothing organically wrong at all. You know as much as I do: she has fever, no appetite, complains of fatigue . . . I am afraid I can find no cause for such symptoms."

"Do you think it may be London? She has not been used to such a pace. We could remove her to Verchamp Park——"

"No; I think a journey would only exacerbate her disorder, though a change of environment might be salubrious. I believe we must wait until the fever breaks; then, perhaps, a removal to the country will be beneficial."

"And is that all? No medicines? No treatment?"

"There are physicians in London," Mr. Whiting answered, "who would prescribe blood-letting, leeching . . . a number of unpleasant procedures. In my opinion, that sort of treatment is useless, and may even be harmful. Your daughter is in no mortal danger; if she is customarily healthy, her body can withstand several days of fasting and fever. Let her rest; let her sleep when she will; offer her tea and broth, but do not press it upon her. Should she fail to recover her appetitie after a few days have passed, we will consider more drastic treatments."

"Is there nothing more I can do for her?" asked Lady Keyes anxiously.

"Only one thing," he replied, smiling slightly. "Go to sleep. You will be of no use to any one if you fall ill yourself."

Mr. Whiting re-entered Daphne's room to brace her with a few cheerful words, but he discovered that she had already dropped off to sleep again, a book still open across her knees. The physician promised to look in on her tomorrow, and took his leave.

Daphne's fever wore on through five more weary days. She slept during most of that time, took water and a very little broth, and fretted, when she was awake to do so, about her mother. Mr. Whiting came each day to examine her; uncertain as to what to do when the fever did not break, he called in a colleague. The gentlemen conferred and decided to delay blood-letting until the following week—by which time, fortunately, Daphne was recovered. Lady Keyes rarely left the sick-room at all. Vases of flowers, novels, and baskets of fruit were sent to Daphne as news that she was ill got round London. She was too fatigued to enjoy any of them, but on the fourth day an enormous basket of roses arrived without a note and Daphne knew they had come from Christian. Her heart beat faster in spite of her condition, and she smiled a little. Then she sank back into sleep again.

Latimer proved himself a most devoted brother during this time, putting himself entirely at his mother's disposal and executing countless commissions. The efficient Mr. Clayton went about his work with sober, troubled eyes, and did his best to keep Sir Latimer distracted. India Ballard called every day, though she could not be admitted to the sick-room, since Mr. Whiting did not know if Daphne's disease was infectious. William Ballard came too, and a good deal of Mr. Clayton's time was spent in dissuading him from trying to send notes up to Miss Keyes which the secretary knew she was too tired to read.

On the morning of the seventh day Daphne awoke with the knowledge that her fever had passed. She was still tired, and she slept during several hours that afternoon, but she was able to take some tea and toast, and to sit up quite cheerfully in bed. Her brother read to her in the evening. The following morning Mr. Whiting consented to allow her visitors, and India Ballard came up.

"This is for you," she said, placing a potted geranium on a table near the windows. "William sent it. I know you won't want it," she went on, surveying the masses of flowers which crowded the bed-chamber, "but William insisted. How are you feeling?"

"Quite well today," said Daphne, patting a place on the bed. "Come and sit by me, my dear."

"You still look dreadful, you know," said India, sitting down on the spot indicated. "O dear, we were terribly worried about you," she cried suddenly, and kissed her friend on the forehead.

"I know," said Miss Keyes, a rueful smile on her lips. "I have put everyone in a pucker. Really, I did not mean to."

"Your mother tells me you will be removing to Verchamp Park soon."

"Yes; Mr. Whiting advises it."

"O well. It is no great matter after all. The Season is nearly at an end."

"Indeed," said Miss Keyes.

"Daphne," said India carefully, "I know it would not be excessively amusing for you, and I know you must miss your home, and I know it is altogether too much to ask—but my parents are getting up a house-party for the early part of the summer: would you come?"

"To Carwaith Abbey?" said Daphne, naming Sir Andrew Ballard's estate in Warwickshire.

"Yes, my dear. It is only the next shire over to yours, so if you don't like it you may leave at any moment. And, of course, Latimer is invited too."

"O India, you are much too good! Of course I should love to come. If my parents will permit me, that is," she added conscientiously.

India smiled broadly and her freckles seemed to dance on her nose. "I have already asked them—do not scold me: I did not wish to trouble you about it if they would not let you go. Latimer has said he will come too, though I think it is mostly for your sake."

"No," Daphne interrupted earnestly; "I believe Latimer is quite fond of William."

"Is he?" asked India. "Well, that's rather odd. Any way, it is all decided. We leave for Carwaith next week; you may travel with us or follow later, as you like."

"O India, what a delightful prospect. You must thank your dear parents for me. Isn't it kind of them to have thought of this party, and to have allowed you to invite Latimer and me? It is very good of them, really."

"I am afraid it is not quite so disinterested in them as

you suppose," said Miss Ballard, a trifle grimly. "Charles Stickney is to be there too, with Dorothea Frane of course. My parents know that Latimer and Charles are friends. I believe they are hoping that with Charles and Dorothea there, so recently betrothed, you know, it will give Lord Midlake ideas."

"Is Lord Midlake to be there as well?" asked Daphne.

Miss Ballard stared at her. "But that is the point of the whole party," she said simply, and dropped her eyes to her hands.

Chapter VII

Lady Bryde took one final sip of tea before setting her cup down. She scrutinised Daphne across the table and apparently approved of what she saw, for she uttered a single "Yes" before relapsing into silence. They were sitting in the breakfast-room at Dome House, a rather cheerful apartment done up with a good deal of white paint and open space. It was Daphne's first excursion into London since her illness, and would be among her last, for she and Latimer were to leave for Carwaith Abbey two days later. Daphne was robed in a walking dress of rose-colored sarsenet; her heavy curls were drawn off her face with rose ribands. She had not yet quite recovered her bloom, but at least she appeared rested, and her countenance had ceased to look pinched. Lady Bryde adjusted one of the pins which anchored her powdered peruke, and spoke again.

"So you're off to Warwickshire, eh girl?" she said. "Your first house-party, is it not?"

"It is."

"Know how to comport yourself?" the Countess demanded, her sharp eyes probing Miss Keyes'.

"I hope so, ma'am."

"So do I." Lady Bryde paused to fix her great-granddaughter's attention. "Occupy yourself until breakfast. Do everything set at your disposal. Do not ask for any thing, do not speak familiarly to their servants, and make it clear that you mean to depart at the end of a fortnight. That way they won't pass their time wondering how to get rid of you. Remember what I have just said and you should have a very acceptable sojourn."

"Thank you," said Daphne.

"O—and one more thing about behaviour. I recall that on my first visit to a country estate, I discovered—quite by chance—that the eldest son of the house had a quite singular attachment to the upper house-maid. In fact, they were involved in a clandestine *affaire d'amour.* I wondered for days whom I ought to tell about it, what I ought to do. Fortunately, I hit upon the correct solution: nothing. If you come upon anything irregular, then, remember to do nothing. No one will thank you, and you certainly have nothing to gain. It may interest you to know, by the way, that that particular eldest son was the Earl of Halston— your great-grandfather. I married him, as you know. I never mentioned the house-maid at all."

Miss Keyes had flushed slightly, but she found nothing to say.

"While I am speaking of marriage, Daphne," the Countess went on, "I think you and I might well have a conference on that head. I have no fear of your brother's chusing an unsuitable wife, when his time comes. He is too vain to marry beneath himself. You, however . . . well, you must tell me yourself. I understand that William Ballard has become quite particular in his attentions towards you."

"I—I suppose he has," Daphne faltered.

"Well, your father tells me he came to Finchley House a week ago to ask permission to solicit your hand. I don't know how much more particular one can become."

The flush on Daphne's cheeks heightened. "I had no notion," she said. "No one mentioned it to me."

"Then he hasn't offered for you yet?" she demanded.

"No. I have hardly seen him since I got well—and we have always been in company. My father gave him permission, then?"

"My poor dear girl, your father would not know how to deny any thing to any one, were it a charwoman asking to eat at his table. Indeed he granted permission—though of course he did not answer for you."

"Well, that is some thing to be grateful for."

"I beg your pardon?" said Lady Bryde, who had never heard her great-grand-daughter speak frankly before.

"I say, I am glad my father did not speak for me. He could not have known what I would say."

"And what would you say, Daphne?" she asked, reflecting silently that perhaps her great-grand-daughter was more like herself than she was used to believe.

"I would thank him for his most flattering offer," she replied, "and tell him No."

"No? A mere No? Not, perhaps, 'I must think on this longer'? Why would you say such a thing?"

"Because I have no desire to marry him, Madam."

"Do you know where you can do better? Has someone else offered for you?"

"No," said Daphne.

"You have not fallen in love, my girl?" the Countess cried sharply.

"No," came the firm reply.

"Then what is it?" Lady Bryde demanded. "He seems a handsome enough lad to me. He is young, clever . . . it is hardly a brilliant alliance, but it is in no way beneath you. Why should you refuse him?"

"Because I do not—" she had been about to say, love him; but she changed her mind. "I do not think he knows me, and I am afraid he will dislike me when he begins to."

"O, if that is all . . . Halston and I scarcely said three

97

words to one another in all the years we were married. He had no more idea of my character than I do of your dog's. What is your dog's name, by the way?"

"Clover."

"Ah yes, Clover. I thought it was something leafy. Any how," she picked up a silver spoon and tapped it idly against her saucer, "if that is your only objection, you have nothing to fear."

"But it is not my only objection, ma'am," Daphne said evenly.

"Out with it, then! Does his taste in clothing repel you? Is he tight-fisted with his money? Is his mother too dominating? What is it?"

"Simply that I have no wish to marry at all. I see no need for it."

Lady Bryde stared at her for a moment, her pale blue eyes wide open. Then she barked a sharp "Ha!" and leaned forward on the table. "You're more foolish than I thought," she said. "I gave you credit for a little wit, but I was wrong."

"I am sorry to disappoint you, ma'am, but I do not know how I have done so."

"Every woman has got to marry," said Lady Bryde, "unless she has a good deal larger fortune than you have, my girl. Marriages like these are what society is made of; they are the only lasting alliances left to us. A woman on her own is under constant scrutiny by her peers; she is suspected and abhorred. The marriage licence, for a woman, is licence to cease living as the prisoner of her parents and to start behaving like a grown person. Doesn't any of that appeal to you?"

"Not especially," said Daphne, shocked at her own candour. "I have never felt the prisoner of my parents, and I am sure they would not wish me to marry to escape them."

"What will you do with your life, my girl?"

"I do not know. Perhaps I shall marry—but not until I feel ready."

The Countess was silent, thinking, for a few moments. She had her own reasons, of course, for wishing Daphne to marry immediately. She had always been a selfish woman, and she did not scruple to act selfishly now. "Daphne," she said at last, "you must think of your father. Verchamp Park is not so prosperous that he could not profit by this alliance. Sir Andrew Ballard is not greatly wealthy, but he has enough at least to settle for a small dowry. Another man will want more. And you must consider the cost to your parents of keeping you at home. It is not the money merely; they are growing older. They must look forward to a time when their children will have set up on their own and the Park will be theirs again. It is your filial duty to marry."

"They never mentioned such a thing," Daphne said weakly.

"Of course they would not." Lady Bryde shook her white head slowly. "Think about it. William Ballard's offer is a good one—perhaps the best you will get. He will give you a comfortable home and, doubtless, plenty of liberty. And India will be your sister-in-law. You like India, don't you?"

"Very much," she agreed.

"Then off you go," said the Countess, rising. "I shall expect to hear news of your betrothal in a very short time." She went to the bell-cord and rang for Hastings. "Show Miss Keyes to the door, please," she instructed. "Then come back to me. Daphne, kiss me good-bye."

Lady Bryde proffered a thin cheek and Daphne kissed it. "I must thank you for all your kindness during this Season," she said.

"Nothing of the sort, child." The Countess gestured

impatiently towards the door. "Nothing of the sort."

When Hastings had returned to the breakfast-room, Lady Bryde requested him to have Cook send up the menu for dinner, so that she might inspect it.

"Very good, Madam," he bowed, his silver head gleaming in the morning light.

"One moment, Hastings," she said as he started away.

"Madam?"

"What do you think about travelling, Hastings? Do you ever get sea-sick?"

"No, Madam." He smiled. "As a lad, I sailed on a merchant vessel."

"Indeed? And where did you go?"

"To the Orient, Madam. I found it very curious."

"But did you like it?" she demanded.

"Very much, my Lady. Will that be all?"

The Countess folded her fragile hands together pensively and dismissed him with a nod. He bowed again and vanished.

The excursion to Vauxhall which had been planned by the Keyes family on the evening of Daphne's falling ill had never been carried out. Sir Latimer suggested that they go there on the eve of his children's departure from London, as a sort of celebration. This proposal being agreeable to every one, Mr. Clayton arranged for a box, and the family set off at about ten o'clock in the evening for the famous Gardens. They found Vauxhall splendidly brilliant, as it always was in those days, the strings of coloured lanterns suspended across the lawns like an hundred rainbows. The occupants of the table at their left happened, quite by chance, to be their friend Lady Mufftow and her party. The Keyes' waited until she noticed them, which she did in due time.

"Lady Keyes!" she cried good-humouredly. "What a delight to see you here. And Sir Latimer, and your charming children." She nodded cheerfully to each of these, her double-chin rolling up and down under her jaw. She had found the various sweetmeats provided by the hostesses of London too great a temptation, and had given up all endeavours to reduce until the Season should be over. She had become, as a result, noticibly plumper, and had chosen to wear black this evening in an effort—only partially successful—to appear slim. Jet black ostrich plumes bobbed atop her turbaned head as she introduced her party to the Keyes'. "You are acquainted with Lord and Lady Trugrove, are you not? And Sir Winifred Glovely, and Lady Frane? Lord Frane is to join us later, you know." She indicated all these briefly and the parties bowed to one another.

Miss Daphne Keyes was not paying attention, nor could she concentrate upon the oyster patties which a waiter had placed before her. Her conciousness, alas, was focused on the other table which adjoined her parents', for one of the diners thereat was Mr. Christian Livingston.

Daphne did not recall ever having seen any of the other members of his party before. There were six at his table in all: himself, two gentlemen, and three ladies. Two of the ladies were apparently married to the unfamiliar gentlemen; the third, a tall, elegant woman of about thirty, had evidently been escorted to Vauxhall by Christian himself. Daphne watched her for a moment. She was making a remark, her white arm—bare except for a narrow bracelet of rubies—held up before her with one tapered finger pointing, as an indication that they must listen to her. What she said must have been witty, for the party broke out in laughter as she spoke, and one of the ladies blushed. Then she turned her graceful blond head towards Christian and whispered something to him.

A dizzy wave surged through Daphne as she made these observations. Lady Mufftow's voice floated into her hearing as if from a great distance. "Yes, it is he," she was saying; "I am positive of it. How extraordinary! One would not have thought that he could find a free evening, what with the way our foremost hostesses have been clamouring to engage him. Who is that lady with him? She is quite a beautiful creature."

"That is Madame la Comtesse des Fîmes," she was informed by Lady Frane. "A clever woman, I am told, but hardly eligible to be received in a London drawing-room. They say she murdered her husband."

"Good Heavens!" Lady Mufftow exclaimed. "What an extraordinary thing to do."

"Of course, it is impossible to make certain of it," Lady Frane added conscientiously.

"Yes, of course," murmured Lady Mufftow. "But still!——"

The ladies went on to discuss the identities of the others at Christian's table, but Daphne did not hear them. She was in the awkward position of facing Christian directly, while he was in profile to her. Thus she could scarcely avoid looking at him, though she knew that at any moment he might turn his head from his companion and see her. She was on the point of begging her mother to exchange places with her, so that her back would be to his table, when he espied her. Her face went absolutely white, but she made no other sign that she had seen him. For his part, he was extremely glad to have this evidence that she was well again, and he smiled genuinely, inclining his head towards her. Still she remained immobile. The moment seemed to endure for hours. When it was done, her colour returned in a rush and she made a push to join the conversation her parents were maintaining. She was excessively glad, when the evening finally ended, to leave Vauxhall.

The family went directly to bed on reaching Finchley House, for Latimer and Daphne meant to depart as early as possible the next morning. Their packing had already been done, and the equipage in which they were to travel prepared. They breakfasted with their parents at noon, said a rather tearful good-bye—for it was the first time they had been separated for any great duration—and began their journey. They went in easy stages, due to Daphne's recent indisposition, and arrived in Warwickshire late the next evening. India met them on the porch of the Abbey.

"I am so glad you've come," she cried, kissing Daphne and shaking her brother's hand cordially. "William has been in all day, wondering when you would get here. He is playing billiards with Charles and my father; Dorothea is in bed with a headache. You do look wonderful, both of you. I cannot tell you how dull the country has been after London." She led the way into the Abbey as she spoke, holding Daphne's hand in her right and gesturing with her left. "I see you've brought no abigail with you, Daphne," she said; "never mind. My Lizzy will do for both of us. Latimer, you may tell your man to follow Frolish; he will know which rooms are meant for you." They were standing in the great front hall of the Abbey now, and Mr. Frolish, who had taken their wraps, bowed to the manservant who had accompanied the Keyes' from London. The two men ascended one side of the double-staircase which led away from the hall, carrying as much of the luggage with them as they could. India, meanwhile, beckoned to her friends and preceded them into the drawing-room, where she invited them to sit down for a moment.

"You will want to freshen up, I know, but you simply must talk to me for a moment before you do so. Are you dreadfully tired? Shall I order you some tea? We are to have supper in an hour."

Brother and sister both accepted the proposed cup of tea gladly; then they sat back to become familiar with their surroundings. The Abbey was a massive structure, its façade obscured by shrubbery and ivy and ornamented all over with a good deal too much in the way of turrets, oriels, and functionless brick-work. The front hall was loftily arched, and indeed all the apartments were high-ceilinged. The double-staircase off the hall had been put in during relatively recent days, and was of creamy marble. The grounds were extensive and included a number of orchards and a formal garden, all very well maintained. The saloon in which they sat now had been done in elegant, lifeless style by the present Lady Ballard, the colours largely muted and drab. Lady Ballard's taste in furniture was so restrained as to be quite Spartan, and this cheerful influence was manifest every where in the interior of the Abbey. It was impossible, she had often remarked, for anything red to be other than ostentatious; that colour, therefore, was entirely shut out of her life, along with most of the other bright hues of the spectrum. As she entered the drawing-room now she did so in a gown of dove-grey, her jewellery onyx set with pearls.

She welcomed the new-comers civilly and offered them tea.

"I've already sent for some, Mother," said India. "Here is Frolish with it now."

Lady Ballard poured the steaming brew and handed it to her daughter's guests. "How are your parents?" she asked.

"Quite well, thank you," said Daphne. "They asked to be remembered to you and Sir Andrew."

"Indeed. Did your mother ever complete that peacock she was embroidering?" inquired her Ladyship.

"Not yet. I am afraid my illness quite overset the household. She will have plenty of time to do it, however, since she and my father mean to return to Verchamp Park next week."

"Of course," said Lady Ballard. "Such a pretty subject to chuse to embroider. So many—ah—vivid colours." She smiled very slightly.

"I will convey your appreciation of it to her when I write to her," Daphne replied.

"Yes, my dear, you must do that. I always was sorry, you know, that you and I never became better acquainted in London. We must do so now."

"I shall be delighted," Miss Keyes murmured.

Evidently, William Ballard had made his plans known to his parents. Daphne turned to Latimer. "I suppose we had best go upstairs, don't you think?" she asked. "We must dress for supper, after all."

Latimer agreed and India offered to escort them to their rooms. This she did, leaving Latimer in an enormous apartment done in brown and ecru, and sitting for a few moments with Daphne.

"You mustn't mind my mother," she said, taking one of the two arm-chairs which had been placed in Daphne's bed-chamber for her convenience. "She means to be amiable, but she has not the least idea how to do it. I was used to detest her when I was younger, but I've learnt to concentrate on her good points. She has several—the foremost of which is that she rarely embarrasses one, at least not by a lack of taste or diplomacy. She is under strictest orders from my father to grow fond of you. William means to marry you, you know."

"So I have been told," said Daphne.

"Are you going to accept him? I should like to be your sister, my dear."

"And I should like to be yours . . . but India, I do not quite know why William should wish to marry me. I have never—favoured him with any thing more than common civility; I have not sought to procure his regard in any way; in fact, there seems to be no particular affinity between us at all—at least, none that I am aware of.'' Daphne rose and began to dress herself in the cream-coloured gown which Lizzy had laid out for her. "To be quite frank, I remember having been positively rude to him on certain occasions—not intentionally, of course, but because I simply could not listen to another flattery. Yet my great-grandmother tells me—and now you tell me again—that he means to marry me. Why? Do your parents press him?"

Miss Ballard stood and went to help Daphne with her buttons. "No," she replied. "The odd thing is, that they do not. I have no doubt that they would, for they have determined that the match is a good one. But William has needed no encouragement. You must remember, my dear, that you are a remarkably pretty girl, that you have a charming manner, and that you are altogether very sweet. Those things alone are enough to attract a gentleman's regard."

"But William is influenced, perhaps, by my birth and fortune as well?"

"Not so much as you suppose, I think. He is sincerely attached to you—though I must say I doubt if he would permit himself to become too attached to any one ineligible to become his wife. We have both been too well brought up to fall into that trap."

Daphne shook her head. "I still do not understand it. I mean—for all the talk one hears of certain gentlemen being great prizes, or certain ladies universally desirable—I have always felt that the important thing is whether two people are suited to one another . . . not merely in rank or wealth, but sympathetically. And I simply cannot believe that any great sympathy lies between William and myself. How could it, unless I were aware of it?"

"Your ideas on the topic of Love are intriguing, as always," India smiled, "but I fear the world proves them wrong. Certain men *are* great catches; and certain ladies are besieged by suitors, some of whom they do not care for at all. But they chuse the most attractive from among them, and this one they marry, and bear children for——"

"And are very unhappy with. Or ignore altogether. I am not persuaded, India. I will not marry any one until I feel our regard and appreciation are mutual. Certainly I should not marry any one whose reasons for loving me were unknown to myself!"

"Then you do not mean to marry William."

"I am afraid I do not," she said gently.

India sighed. "It will disappoint him," she said.

"I am learning that it is very easy to disappoint certain people," Daphne replied. A few moments later they went down to supper.

"Where is Lord Midlake?" Miss Keyes inquired, as they went, stopping to collect Latimer and then proceeding with him.

"O, that is quite a nightmare," India said, pulling a grotesque face in which many emotions mingled. "He is here, but he keeps to his room almost constantly. My parents are in despair, and to say truth it makes me a bit uncomfortable as well. I doubt if he will come to supper."

"Perhaps he is ill?" Latimer suggested.

"A cheerful supposition," sighed India, "but one, alas, which has no base in truth. No, I fear that my Lord simply regrets ever having agreed to come here at all, and keeps his solitude until he finds means to escape."

"If that is so, your parents will be doubly disappointed," said Daphne, casting an anxious glance at her brother, before whom she felt she ought not to be discussing William's offer.

"I see what you mean," India agreed; "but there is nothing to be done, after all."

"I do not see what you mean," said Latimer. Daphne said nothing. "O very well, keep your secrets. Tell me if I am properly dressed instead. Do you like my quizzing-glass?" He lifted the heavy ornament which dangled from beneath his waist-coat.

"It is very elegant," Daphne approved.

He smiled, immeasurably pleased. "I chose it myself," he informed her, "without asking any one's opinion. I think it is an unusually handsome one."

"It is. And you are unusually handsome yourself," said Daphne, giving him a hasty kiss.

"My cravat!" he protested.

The three of them entered the dining-parlour laughing.

After supper there was whist. Dorothea Frane's headache improved, and she came down to play a round of Consequences with the other young people. Latimer and Daphne, still weary from the journey, went early to bed, and the others followed soon after. Lord Midlake did not make a public appearance until next afternoon; but when he did, a rather extraordinary scene ensued.

Chapter VIII

It was a little before three o'clock. Lady Ballard, thinking that the young people might be hungry after the ride they had taken during the morning, had ordered a nuncheon served in the Eastern Parlour, a hexagonal chamber of staggering dimensions. Frolish was sent, as always, to apprise Lord Midlake that a collation was available to him should he care to take anything, and he—after pulling mightily on his long left ear for a moment—decided to come down. Walter Midlake was a peaceable man. His desires were few, his satisfactions many; altogether, his life suited him very well. He knew India Ballard had been setting her cap at him all last Season, and all the year before, but he felt no special inclination to marry— especially as he had numerous younger brothers, to whom the title might as well go. Sir Andrew had tempted him to Carwaith Abbey with the promise of some good riding and some acceptable fishing; and as he had no other plans, he had accepted the invitation. Generally, one place suited him as well as another; however, even he had found Lady Ballard's attempts to get him to take notice of her daughter a bit too much to ignore, and had consequently removed himself from the house-party as frequently as possible. He decided, however, as he pulled on his ear, that he did have something of an appetite just now, and this prosaic perception was responsible for his appearance in the Eastern Parlour shortly afterwards.

He greeted Daphne and Latimer equably, asked Stickney who had won at billiards last night, inquired after Miss Frane's health, and helped himself to some ham. Lady Ballard watched him closely through all of this, but did not say any thing until he had done eating. Then she sat down by him on a narrow sofa and asked "if there were any thing more she could bespeak for him?"

"No," said Midlake. "I am quite content, thank you. Jolly good jam-puffs you've got there."

"India makes them herself," said her Ladyship.

Lord Midlake chewed on his lower lip.

"As for myself, I never could see what amusement there might be in cooking, but India haunts the kitchens constantly."

Lord Midlake chewed on his upper lip.

"She looks pale, today, I think," Lady Ballard went on. "I asked her to take some exercise, but she would not ride out with the others. She does not care for riding, you know."

"Indeed," said his Lordship.

"No, not very much. She will walk in the garden, some times, but usually not unless someone invites her to do so. I would go with her myself, except that I've got so much correspondence to take care of. Isn't it dreadful the way one's letters pile up!"

"Very dreadful " agreed Lord Midlake, chewing his lower lip again and pulling hard on one long ear.

"I don't suppose you would care for a walk in the garden today?" suggested my Lady.

"O, on the contrary; I think I should indeed," Lord Midlake conceded at last. "Perhaps Miss Ballard will be kind enough to come with me." He breathed an heavy sigh.

Lady Ballard smiled. "I think she might. You must ask her yourself, though," she added.

"Yes, yes . . . pardon me." Lord Midlake rose and went to do as he was bid, the drooping corners of his mouth conveying resignation, if nothing else. Miss Ballard, of course, accepted his kind offer, and when the others went off to investigate the cellars of the Abbey—for they were extensive, and had rarely been explored in recent times—she and Walter Midlake walked out into the formal gardens.

These gardens were set out in a succession of rectangles, six or seven in all, which lay endwise to the Abbey and stretched almost to the edge of a little spinney beyond them. In the most distant of the rectangles was a small, ornamental pool; they had reached this place and stood beside it, talking, when the extraordinary incident occurred.

"O my," said Miss Ballard, suddenly. "I do feel queer." She put a hand to her forehead and pressed it to her temples.

"Perhaps you ought to sit down," said Lord Midlake, indicating the low wall which surrounded the pool.

"O no—I do not think so . . . it will pass in a moment," said she, breathing in very short breaths and blanching slightly beneath her freckles.

"Do you often have such symptoms?" Midlake was asking, when all at once, India fainted dead away in the direction of his arms. Lord Midlake had been about to pull on his right ear, but he stretched his arms out in time to catch her, and for a few instants stood there holding her with not the slightest notion what to do. As she gave no sign of recovering, it struck him that he might as well take her back to the Abbey, where some one could attend to her; and as she could not walk, he carried her. Thus it was that when the party of explorers emerged (disappointed in their search for any thing mysterious) from the cellars, they were greeted with the rather unusual spectacle of Lord Midlake with an unconscious young woman in his arms. Lady Ballard had seen him approaching through the gardens and had run out onto the terrace; now she directed him to carry India up to her bed-chamber, begging him to do so carefully, and appearing on the edge of a swoon herself. The concern of the erstwhile explorers was voiced in a score of anxious questions, none of which was answered. Lord Midlake, utterly confounded at finding himself the center of all this excitement, bit his lips vigorously and carried the seemingly lifeless damsel upstairs. Lady Ballard followed a little ways behind, and Daphne dared to follow her.

As Walter Midlake reached the upstairs corridor, wondering all the time how he was to open her bed-room door, should it prove to be closed, India's eyelids began to flutter and she moaned faintly. "Miss Ballard?" said he, tentatively.

"What—where . . . O, Walter," she said weakly, her green eyes opening fully to gaze into his.

"Yes, yes . . . Midlake, Walter Midlake," he reminded her. "Can you walk?"

He would have set her down, but she clung to him. "No . . . my bed . . . please," she murmured. Her fluttering lids closed again.

His Lordship, finding the door to her chamber ajar, obliged her. Her left hand grasped his shoulder loosely as he set her on the bed and slid easily down to his wrist. He was starting to go to the door again, to see where Lady Ballard could be, when her hand, miraculously reanimated, gripped his. "Don't—go," she whispered.

Helpless, he stood by the bed and watched as her eyes re-opened. A tremulous smile came to her lips and she said softly, "You are so kind to help me."

"It is—er—nothing, really. Nothing at all."

"O no," she insisted. "You must have carried me . . . all the way from the garden. Was I terribly heavy?"

"No, not at all, Light, in fact."

The smile became more certain of itself. "So sweet of you . . . to say so."

Lord Midlake tugged at his ear with his free hand and turned towards the door-way. "Your mother——" he began.

"O yes, she will come soon to fuss over me, no doubt. But—Walter, will you think me mad if I tell you . . . I am almost glad it happened. Yes, glad. I had no idea how capable you were . . . so strong." She cast one last adoring glance at his bewildered eyes and turned her head away from him on the pillow. "I must—rest now," she murmured.

"Ah—indeed," said he. At this juncture Lady Ballard swept in, a vinaigrette in one hand and her demi-train in the other. Lord Midlake's relief at her arrival was exquisite, in spite of the fact that India still had not let go his hand, thus forcing him to stand by the bed holding it awkwardly.

"What ever occurred?" asked Lady Ballard in an urgent whisper as she held the vinaigrette to the freckled nose of her moaning daughter.

"Why, nothing. I don't know. We were standing by the pool, and the next moment she fainted. I've no idea," he repeated.

Lady Ballard fixed him with a distrustful look, distrust being an emotion which her cold features easily expressed. "You said nothing to shock her?" she asked.

"Nothing at all, I assure you. We were talking, I believe of——O dear, what was it? Of hedges! Yes, I think it was hedges."

"Hedges indeed," sniffed her Ladyship. "An interesting topic."

"But we were, I assure you——" he began miserably.

"I wish you will stop assuring me and do something useful," she returned. "Why do you hang about my daughter, upsetting her like this? She is very delicate; her sentiments cannot be toyed with!" Her low voice whispered harshly as she took India's hand to rub it. "At one time, we thought you wished to secure her affections, and were courting her; then we heard nothing from you for months. Three week ago, at Dorothea Frane's ball, you paid her the most particular attention . . . but a bare se'ennight later you refused an invitation to dine with us, and cut her in the Park. Now you are here again, and I am sure I do not know why." India was beginning to recover: she turned her head on the pillow, though her eyes were still shut. "I am sorry to be forced to speak so frankly, sir," Lady Ballard hissed, "but I cannot sit idly by while my daughter's heart is played with. I really must beg you, my Lord, to inform us as to your intentions towards her, or to leave the Abbey at once."

India stirred again. "Mamma?" she said.

"Yes, my dear, I am here," said she, stroking her hand.

"Mamma, I am so shaken . . ."

"You see what I mean," said Lady Ballard to Lord Midlake. "The poor girl is deeply troubled. I think you had better go now; we can resume this conversation later, if necessary."

Lord Midlake would have excused himself, but as soon as he opened his mouth he began to stutter, and could not stop. Instead, he pulled at both ears simultaneously and bowed, after which he quitted the room.

He met Daphne in the corridor, who asked him anxiously if he thought she might go in. He said nothing—

since he could not—and she, taking his silence for an affirmative, entered the room he had just left. An astonishing conversation was taking place.

India was sitting up in bed, her colour entirely restored, looking in fact the picture of health. "It cannot have failed," she was saying. "You were quite splendid!"

Lady Ballard shrugged off this praise, answering, "So long as it works; that is the important thing."

"We ought to know soon enough, after the performance you——O Daphne," she interrupted herself, "did you see what Mother has done? Was she not splendid?" She rose from the bed and began to straighten out her rumpled skirt.

"I beg your pardon?" said Miss Keyes. "I hope I am not intruding, but I was concerned . . ."

"Did you think——? O dear, it is too amusing! You see how well it was done, Mother; even Daphne did not know."

"Did not know what?" Daphne persisted. "India, I thought you had fainted."

"That is what you were meant to think, my dear silly girl. Or rather, it is what Lord Midlake was meant to think. I am sure he did—and after the tongue-lashing Mother just gave him—O, famous!"

"Then you were not ill at all?"

"No, of course not." India sounded a trifle irritated. "The point was to put Lord Midlake into an awkward position—to get him to offer for me, you know. O, and I believe we have succeeded very well, better than I had dared to hope."

Daphne was quite aghast, though she did her best not to show it. "Well, if you are not ill . . . then I suppose I ought to join the others. I am glad you are well, at least. What shall I tell them?"

"O, that I will keep to my bed for a few hours, though I

seem some what better. That should answer, shouldn't it ma'am?'' she asked her mother.

"Yes, that will do very well. Poor Daphne must think our behaviour extraordinary, but you must try to understand how vexatious this business with Lord Midlake has been to us. We have had no question but that he meant to offer for India; it is only his wretched indecision which has kept him from it. This—little deception—will prove a help to him in the long run, I promise you."

"O, Mother, Daphne is not the sort to moralise. She is not at all missish. You needn't explain to her."

Lady Ballard smiled condescendingly. "Nonetheless, I think I must go with her to inform the others of your state of health," she said firmly. "I will have your dinner sent up to you, India. Don't come down until nine, at the earliest. Now Daphne, come with me," she added, taking her arm and leading her to the door. "India will be able to amuse herself until this evening."

Daphne followed her obediently.

The party separated into little groups during the remainder of the afternoon: Daphne and Latimer wrote a long, joint letter to their parents; Lord Midlake retired with Sir Andrew into the latter's study; Dorothea and Charles announced their intention to read in the library, but no one particularly believed them. Lady Ballard was contemplating having a carriage designed for her own use, and she requested her son's assistance in this matter. At six-thirty every one went to dress for dinner, at which repast they met an hour later.

Conversation at the table was easy and gay, despite the concern of certain of the persons present for India's health. Daphne had wished to discuss the perplexing deception which she had stumbled upon with Latimer, but she remembered Lady Bryde's warning and kept silent. Charles Stickney had recently acquired a small property in Kent, where he and Dorothea planned to begin their life together, and this topic and related ones were much discussed. India joined the ladies after they had retired to the drawing-room, professing her health to be much improved and darting inquiring looks at her mother. These glances Lady Ballard returned with a slow nod and an exceedingly satisfied smile. India smiled too.

The gentlemen joined them in due course and Lady Ballard excused herself to complete the correspondence which she had meant to attend to that afternoon. Lord Midlake was looking positively green, but he suggested to Miss Ballard that she might like to take a turn on the terrace. Miss Ballard agreed. Sir Andrew proposed a game of billiards to Latimer, who accepted eagerly. Charles and Dorothea remained for a short while in the drawing-room, but then Miss Frane remembered something which she had left in the library, and said she must fetch it. Mr. Stickney offered to accompany her there, and the two of them disappeared.

All of which left Daphne alone with William.

She had been fearing this encounter greatly, and trying to avoid it, but none of the activities proposed by the others was the sort of scheme into which one could intrude oneself very conveniently. Her hopes that William might decide to join his father at billiards were soon dashed, and she had been forced to sit helplessly while two by two the company vanished. She attempted to rise now on a pretext, but William restrained her.

"Don't go; I beg you will not," he said.

"But I really ought——"

"It cannot be so important. I have been hoping to be alone with you since you arrived, but somehow it has been impossible."

"Why should you wish to be alone with me?" she asked, with unconvincing naïveté.

"Only to tell you how beautiful you are."

"O dear," said she, her alarm genuine.

"Yes, and to say how much I admire your charm, your vivacity, your quick, clever disposition——"

"O dear," she said again.

"But you must listen!" he pleaded, as she turned away from him. They sat several feet apart on a settee of so dark a blue as to appear black. William reached for her hand, but she withdrew it and placed it in her lap with the other, folding and unfolding them nervously. "It is such exquisite relief to me to be allowed to vent my feelings thus," William continued. "I must tell you . . . with what deep affection I regard you, how profoundly I care for you——"

"For Heaven's sake!" she cried suddenly. "You do not know me!"

"But I do know you," said he earnestly, moving closer to her and reaching again for her hand. She snatched it away. "I do know you. I know your whims, your tastes; I have made a study of them, India has told me everything. Your favourite colour is blue; you are partial to raspberries; you prefer poetry to prose——O, and you are so utterly adorable!" he broke off, kneeling (to her absolute horror) before her. "Say you will be my wife, I beg it. Say you return my regard!"

"I do—I do not . . . I hardly know what . . . O for the love of Heaven Itself, *will* you get up off your knees?" she exclaimed at last. "How is any one to think with some one grovelling before her?"

William was annoyed at her mistaking his supplicating posture for "grovelling," but he stood up and sat down again beside her and did not allow himself to be swayed from his purpose. "Say at least that I hold a place in your sentiments; say at least that!"

"Well, that is easy to say," she replied, thinking how

perfectly preoccupied her emotions now were with trying not to injure his pride.

"Ah, that is some thing!" he cried, attaining her hand at last.

"But no, it is nothing," she contradicted. "O dear, I *wish* you will not press your suit on me thus——"

"I spoke too soon," he interrupted. "I was afraid I might; forgive me, I pray. Say you do not entirely despise me."

"No of course I do not. I do not entirely despise any——"

"But say you will allow me to address you again," he broke in once more. "Say that!"

"But this is ridiculous!"

"O, not ridiculous; do not call it so, I implore you. My dear Miss Keyes——" he began again to sink to his knees, but remembered she did not care for that in time to stop himself "—these decisions are too significant to be made in a single night. Say you will think of it; say I may ask you again; say you will consider it, please."

Daphne's face was suffused with colour. She felt very foolish, not a little confused, and extremely embarrassed for him as well as for herself. "I——O dear," she faltered finally, "I will." She was sorry as soon as she said it.

"You have made me very happy," said he, in reverent tones. "From now until we speak alone again, I live only for my hopes, my prayers, my dreams."

"Dreams indeed," she murmured grimly. Happily, he did not hear her, being in the act of showering kisses upon her hand. When at last he had done with that, he stood up, and she was allowed to go.

At supper, India announced her betrothal to Lord Midlake. Her pale cheeks were flushed with triumph, and his sallow ones with mortification at all the attention being paid them. They were felicitated and toasted roundly, especially by Dorothea Frane, who came forward shyly to hope "they would be as happy as she and Charles were." Daphne found her feelings profoundly divided. On the one hand, she was glad to know that India had achieved her professed aim; on the other, she doubted very much whether Miss Ballard really wanted what she thought she did. In any case, there was no question of Daphne's doing any thing about it, so she assumed a wide smile and wished them very happy. Certainly, she did wish that.

There was a good deal of wine drunk, and several speeches were made in a jubilant vein. Latimer got quite bosky—in earnest, this time—as did William Ballard. When the company had grown tired of toasting India and Walter, they began to toast Charles and Dorothea; and when they had grown weary of that, young William apparently could not bear to see the festive spirit fade. For this reason, as well as because he was slightly intoxicated, he stood up at his place at the supper-table and made what was for Daphne a most embarrassing, even shocking, announcement.

"My dear friends, my dear family," called he, tapping a glass with his coffee-spoon to attract their attention, "it is my very, very deep pleasure to add to this celebration a hint of future happiness. Miss Daphne Keyes has this evening promised—not to marry me—but to think of it." He cast an excited glance at Daphne's crimson face. "I know you will join me in my hopes that she will answer, when she answers, in the affirmative." With that he sat down, amid polite applause. His announcement was not nearly so well received as the earlier one; in fact, Sir Andrew felt his move was impolitic, and Lady Ballard would dearly have loved to box his ears. India, too, was more surprised than delighted to hear this unexpected news of her friend, but no one knew how to unsay William's words, so they did the next best thing, which was to ignore them as much as possible.

Daphne herself was furious. It occurred to her that William was consciously attempting to coerce her into accepting his suit in the same way that Lady Ballard had coerced Lord Midlake. Whether or not this was so, she was in a raging passion by the time he finished his speech, and it was all she could do not to jump up and contradict his every word. After all the effort she had spent trying to conciliate him! After being at such pains to spare him embarrassment! She made sure of one thing in her mind, if she did not do so aloud: she would not allow herself to be forced into any such betrothal; in fact, she would not allow herself to be forced even to speak to him, were she ever so rude in avoiding him. She excused herself from the supper-table early, wishing all the while that Latimer were not so drunk. If he had been sober she would have begged him to come up to her room, so that she could vent her spleen to some one. As it was, however, he was in a haze of euphoria, and would make a very unsatisfactory confidant indeed.

While Daphne paced her room angrily, wondering whether or not to leave Carwaith Abbey at once, her brother hit upon a notion which was destined, though he could not know this, to prove infelicitous in the extreme. Rising from the table soon after Daphne herself, he went to Sir Andrew's study and made use of that gentleman's pen and ink to write a letter. It was to his parents, and the fateful phrase ran thus: "William Ballard announced tonight that he has offered for Daphne and that she is considering his suit; everyone expects that she will accept him soon, as there seems to be good reason to believe that she will." This missive he then sealed and handed into the care of Frolish, who put it with the other letter the Keyes' had written that day. Long before Daphne was awake to learn of it, it had been sent.

When at last every toast had been made that any one could imagine, the supper-table was abandoned and the company returned to calmer pursuits. Lord Midlake complained of a slight queasiness—due to having drunk a bit too much, no doubt—and retired early to bed after kissing his betrothed dutifully. She, already more than sated with his company for one day, turned this opportunity to good account by slipping upstairs herself and paying a visit to Daphne. The two young women had much to discuss.

India refused to admit that she was otherwise than thoroughly content with her new future. "You do not know how it has been for me, my dear," she said. "Time was running out. I am not old, but I am certainly not young; and I think you have seen enough of my parents by now to know how inviting the prospect of eternity with them appears to me. Midlake will be better by far—by far, I assure you."

"I am glad you still feel so," Daphne returned. "I only hope you may continue to."

"I will; don't fret. But now I think you must tell me what has gone on between you and William! That was rather a bizarre announcement he made tonight."

Daphne had made a space in her rage to consider her friend's circumstances, but now her blood surged up again and she fairly spat her words. "Bizarre! I should think so. Insane comes closer; ungentlemanly, tactless, idiotic, self-defeating, insufferable . . . any of those, all of them! India, you know how dearly I love you, and you must believe how little I should like to quarrel with you—but your brother's behaviour tonight has passed all bounds." She paused, not because she had no more to say, but because too many words were burning her tongue for her to chuse among them.

"I was afraid of that," India said simply. "I did not think you would have changed your mind so quickly."

"I have not changed my mind at all. Your brother talked to me at such length, and in such terms, that to promise him any thing less than to think of him seemed like murder, at the time."

"I suppose you wish now you *had* murdered him," India sighed.

"I am afraid I do."

"Yes. Well, you mustn't feel badly. I know exactly what you are talking about. This isn't the first time William has tried to bully people about . . . he doesn't mean to, you know. It's just his way."

"He might try to govern it."

"He gets it from my father."

They were both silent for a moment. "I won't give in, you know," Daphne said fiercely.

"No, of course you must not. Try not to loath him, however; he probably believes you are sincerely attached to him, and are only too shy to admit it. I know it seems incredible, but hordes of men think that about the most unlikely women."

"Yes. Well," said Daphne. An instant later, when she felt her anger die quite away, she confided sheepishly, "I was thinking of leaving the Abbey at once. Of course I will not now."

"O no, you cannot!" cried India. "There is some thing you do not know . . . I have been saving it for the right moment. I'm not sure this is quite the sort of moment I had envisioned, but—well, you are aware that William is about to reach his majority, of course."

"Yes," said Daphne, puzzled. "On the fifth, is it not?"

"Exactly. And you are aware, too, that my parents have been planning a large celebration of the event?"

"Yes; you told me so yourself once. Any way, your mother mentioned this evening that she meant to turn it into a double celebration—for you and Lord Midlake. But I do not see——"

"You will in a moment. O Daphne, I don't know whether I will make you angry when I tell you this, but my mother suggested to me, while we were still in London, that we engage the services of a really good pianofortist. She asked me whom I should chuse myself, and I—O my dear friend, don't bite me when I tell you this—but I proposed Mr. Christian Livingston. He is coming here next week."

Chapter IX

News among the *ton* travels rapidly, even when—one might almost say, particularly when—it is not quite true. No sooner had Lady Keyes received her son's brief post script to the earlier, longer letter, than she sat down at her writing-table and scribbled a note to her grandmother. It was delivered to the drawing-room of Dome House not two days later, and when Lady Bryde had opened it, and had made her way through the courteous salutation, the polite inquiries, and the requisite mention of every one's health, she came to the following:

> Having had two letters from Carwaith Abbey today, I am delighted to be able to inform you that the match you had hoped to see made between Daphne and William Ballard is well on its way to successful completion. I must confess, dear ma'am, that you were right to press us to visit London, since it has brought so many people so much happiness.

Below this was another paragraph, concerned mainly with the bailiff of Verchamp Park, who had succumbed to a fit of apoplexy and had to be replaced, and then the formal closing of the letter, which was almost so long as to make a paragraph in itself.

Lady Bryde folded the letter and tucked it into the

volume she had been reading—a book entitled *Travels through Africa,* by a Mrs. Hodgeson. The expression on her withered countenance was one of delicious anticipation. She rang for Hastings, who came immediately, and invited him (for the first time in his thirty years of service to her) to sit down. The interview which ensued, behind the closed doors of the drawing-room, lasted about two hours.

Lady Bryde had a very clear mental image, while she did these things, of what scenes must be going forward at Carwaith Abbey. As it happened, the dramas she imagined were very far from the true case. Daphne, instead of being absorbed in pleasant reverie about her future life with William, was entirely preoccupied with Christian Livingston, whose arrival was imminent. She had interrogated India a score of times regarding him: "Did Mr. Livingston know Miss Keyes was to be at the Abbey?"

India was not certain.

"Was Mr. Livingston expected to stop at Carwaith for any length of time after the celebration?"

India believed so.

"How long, then?"

Miss Ballard would ask her mother—who said that, of course, he would stay as long as any of the guests, since that was the custom in these things.

"Were there guests who meant to stay long?"

Lord and Lady Frane were expected to stop a week.

"Ought Miss Keyes to leave the Abbey directly, before he came—in spite of the odd impression it would give?"

Miss Ballard would never forgive her.

"Well then, was she quite certain there was no means of finding out whether Mr. Livingston knew Miss Keyes would be there?"

"For Heaven's sake, Daphne!" cried India, when her

friend had asked this question for perhaps the hundredth time. "If he does not know you are with us, you may be certain he soon will."

"But India," said Miss Keyes in distress, "what will he say to it? How shall I behave towards him? I gave him the cut direct, you know, at Vauxhall."

"Very likely he did not even notice."

"He could not help but notice."

"Then he will pardon you. He will understand."

"How can he, when I do not understand myself?"

"My dear Daphne, we must try to sort this thing out. Now precisely what do you want from Mr. Livingston? Will you be happy to see him?"

"I don't—O dear, truly I do not know. In London, just before my illness, I made sure I never wished to see him again."

"But now you think perhaps you would like to."

"Yes—that is, no. No, India, I cannot see him. I swore an oath that I would not."

"Indeed?" she asked, surprised. "To whom?"

"To myself."

"O, well if that is all . . . why did you do such a thing?"

"Because I cannot believe he wishes me well; because if he were a friend to me, he would not have proposed such a painful . . . I do not even know what to call it."

"But I am a friend to you, and I proposed just the same thing."

"Yes, but that is different. You are—I understand you better. You are a woman. You can have no . . . no unspoken motive."

"And can he?"

"But of course! He——" she faltered.

"Come my dear," said India, taking her hand and leaning towards her. "There is a carriage in the drive and I

believe it must be Charles' parents. I ought to go and greet them, but before I do, let me say one last word. Christian Livingston is a pianofortist. He has been engaged to play here by my parents. If you do not like to, there is no need whatever for you to speak to him. If you find you should like to, however—if you find yourself drawn to him, well then go to him. He has nothing to gain by a liaison with you except the mutual pleasure it will afford both of you. Of course you must do nothing—decisive—until you are married . . . and my dear, you really might consider marrying William, under the circumstances. He is not a bad fellow, after all, and it would make him very happy."
Daphne was about to protest, but India continued before she could speak. "But if you still do not like the idea, then refuse him. Mr. Livingston will wait, and when you do marry—as I am sure you will—you may pursue your acquaintance with him then. There, that is all I have to say on that head, and I sincerely hope you will stop fretting about it. I really must go and meet the Stickneys now . . . forgive me for running off." On these words she rose, leaving Daphne alone.

Mr. Livingston arrived on the day following this conversation. Very little fuss was made over him, since the Earl and Countess of Colworth had driven up five minutes before him, and Lady Ballard's cousin Clarissa descended from her coach five minutes later. Lady Ballard received them all equally; Frolish and the footmen under him ran up- and down-stairs all day, arranging baggage and instructing the various servants who accompanied their employers as to the location of the kitchens, the stables, and the back-stairs. The great celebration was to take place tomorrow; in all, about sixteen persons, not counting the house-party, sat down to supper that evening. Those who lived close enough to the Abbey to make it feasible would arrive the next day; very few were the guests who could manage to come and go on the evening of the gala itself. Carwaith simply teemed with people, but Lady Ballard was nothing if not a competent hostess and she never once forgot herself. Every detail had been planned, and every thing went on as she had foreseen—except that one place at the supper-table was empty, and had to be removed. That place, of course, belonged to Daphne, who had kept to her room ever since Christian's arrival. India had warned her that he would be treated, in general, as a guest (since this was a country house)—which meant that he would take his meals with the others. The fact that "the others" did not include Miss Keyes tonight disturbed William Ballard more than any one else; Mr. Livingston had noticed Latimer, but he did not know that his sister was with him.

It did occur to him, however, that she might be, and he took pains after supper to discover if it were so. Several of the guests had gone directly to bed, being fatigued from travel; a number of them lounged about the billiard-room and not a few strolled through the gardens. Mr. Livingston—whose status in the present circumstances was so unclear that very few of the invited guests knew whether, or how, to talk to him—wandered alone from the supper-room into the Eastern Parlour, where he found, among others, Mr. Latimer Keyes. He hesitated before addressing the younger man: his position in the company was as murky to him as it was to any of the others, a fact which he found most disconcerting. He reasoned at last, however, that if Lady Ballard expected him to dine with the others, she must also expect him to become acquainted with her guests; arming himself with this logic, he tapped Latimer on the shoulder.

"I beg your pardon?" said Latimer, turning. "O, it is you. Aren't you the fellow who——"

"I am Christian Livingston," said he.

"Ah yes. I don't believe I've actually had the pleasure——"

"No, I think not. You must pardon me for introducing myself," he went on, "but I thought I recognised your face. You are Mr. Keyes, are you not?"

"I am," said he, pleased to have been remembered.

"I would have asked our hostess—or rather, your hostess—to introduce us, but she has been so very occupied."

"Indeed," Latimer agree. He had been standing, with several others, round a young nephew of Sir Andrew's who had produced a number of curious playthings made of wood and phosphorous, which he called matches. They made a flame when struck against any thing rough, and were quite fascinating, though apparently useless. Now Latimer detached himself from the group and stood a little apart with Mr. Livingston, who was some six inches taller than himself and looked down upon him amiably. "You are to play tomorrow night, sir?" he asked.

Mr. Livingston bowed. "To say truth, I am a little at a loss for what to do with myself now, however. I am not accustomed to being among Society except when my services are required. This is the first time I have played any where but in London; it is rather confusing."

"Really? The first time? Then you have never been to a country affair before?" asked Latimer, as if he had been to dozens of them.

"Never at all," Christian agreed. "Are you a friend of Master Ballard's, or a relative——?"

"O, I do not think they would have invited me if it had not been for Daphne—my sister, that is. She is a bosom bow of Miss Ballard's, you know, and," he lowered his voice to a whisper, "it looks as if she is about to accept William. He offered for her yesterday."

This information affected Christian strongly, and in

several ways. First of all, he was inexpressibly delighted to learn that Daphne was indeed present; he had been entirely unaware that she might be, for though he had been lucky enough to overhear that she was leaving London, he could not discover where she had gone. Along with the pleasure of that, however, came the rather grating news that she might be about to marry. Though he had counselled her to do so himself, he could not quite be glad about it. Lastly, it occurred to him that she might be marrying precisely because he had advised it, in which case . . . the possibilities were enormously intriguing, and he found himself consumed with curiosity. "Is that so?" he answered politely, as if it were nothing to him. "I am not certain I have met your sister . . . where did she sit at supper?"

"O, she was not at supper at all. I suppose you cannot have met her, if you thought she was."

"Quite so. I hope she is not unwell?"

"No—at least, I do not think so. I believe she has the headache, and wished to sup alone. Nothing serious, though, or I am sure she would have told me."

"Of course," said Christian.

"I say, didn't you play at her come-out? I don't go in much for music myself, but I could have sworn it was you."

Mr. Livingston smiled. "It may well have been. I played at so many come-outs this Season, I could not really be certain."

"O well. No doubt when you see her you will remember if you did—or perhaps she will," said Latimer carelessly.

"Yes. Perhaps she will." Mr. Livingston smiled again, bowed, and excused himself. He went into the drawing-room to try the key-board of the Abbey's elegant pianoforte, which was of oak, with mahogany and tulipwood marquetry. After a few minutes, during which he tried to become accustomed to its action, he realized suddenly how tired he was and went up to bed. He was disappointed, when morning came, to find that Daphne had not come down to breakfast; he sat again at the instrument in the drawing-room to stretch his fingers a bit and to while away the hours until she should appear.

Upstairs, Daphne was in an agony of indecision. It happened that her bed-chamber was fixed just above the entrance to the Abbey. Looking down on the previous day, she had seen Christian enter. The knowledge that he was so close to her—even though made inaccessible by her own scruples—filled her with a strange jubilance, then an uncontrollable trembling. She was astonished to find, as she stood at the window and watched him disappear into the house, that her heart actually hurt—indeed, ached. It was dreadful to know that the mere sight of him could affect her so deeply, in spite of all her resolutions, in spite of the pain she had undergone since their last meeting, in spite of her illness, and in spite of having cut him dead at Vauxhall. What was it? Her mind freely admitted that she knew little of him indeed, yet her body seemed to strain towards his, and her spirit—this was worst of all—still had not learnt to blush at this most uninvited passion. She did not feel, nor had she ever felt, any shame in her love for him. In vain the remonstrances of conscience; in vain the arguments of reason . . . "Le coeur a ses raisons, que la raison ne connaît point," says Pascal, and Daphne's heart during the long night of Christian's arrival proved much wiser than the discourse of her logic. She did not come down to breakfast because she wished to meet him alone, and when she did appear at last it was to gaze at him across the empty drawing-room with eyes heavy from sleeplessness and a heart weary with mute conflict.

He was playing the Andante movement of a sonata he

had composed himself; his eyes, which had been straying blindly towards the French doors of the drawing-room, caught her movement as she entered and came to rest on her. For a moment his fingers slowed on the ivory keys; then he returned his attention to them and completed the remaining measures of the Andante. It was a sweet, sad melody, with a melancholy theme which echoed and re-echoed through many variations. She closed the doors soundlessly behind her and crossed the room to him, as if drawn by the rich, sombre music. When he had done he took his hands from the keys and gave them to her, and for a long moment they looked at one another in silence.

A thousand phrases passed through her mind. She wanted to apologise for having doubted him, for having cut him, for being unable even now to forgive him fully. His long, slender fingers entwined with hers, and she said nothing. At last he bent his gleaming blond head to her hands, held them within his, and kissed them. Lifting his liquid green eyes to her own dark ones, he stood and kissed her forehead, her eyelids, her lips. He kissed her as one plucks petals from a flower: delicately, indolently, with a tremor as if stealing from the gods. She returned his embrace and felt his heart beat against hers.

"You are tired," he whispered, noticing her pale cheeks and the shadows beneath her eyes. "Are you ill again? I was worried."

"No, Christian," she replied. "I think I shall be well now."

He smiled and they stood a little apart from one another, their hands still joined. "You are brave to come to me here, but it is not wise."

"I do not care."

"But you must care."

She sighed. "Very well then, I will begin to care."

"Say you will meet me in the farthest garden, by the

pool, at four o'clock. We may slip into the woods beyond it, and no one will see us. Here, any one may walk in."

"How practised you are in these arrangements," she said.

"How cruel you are to remark upon it."

"How hard we have both been to one another," she said in a low voice.

"We will make up for it."

She did not answer—merely bowed her head and quitted the room—but at four o'clock she met him by the still pool. He had gone there earlier, and awaited her.

"Did you have much trouble in slipping away?" he asked.

"No." She had been obliged to lie to Latimer in order to leave the Abbey, but it pained her so much even to think of this that she did not wish to mention it.

Christian looked round. A few figures were visible in the garden plot closest to the building, but they were too distant for him to make out their identities. Satisfied that they were not observed, he took Daphne's hand and led her towards the small spinney. To leave the garden it was necessary to cross over the low border of shrubbery which enclosed it; Daphne tripped on the hem of her skirt as she reached the far side. He caught her, saying, "You are not hurt?"

"No." It was a second falsehood: in fact, she had twisted her ankle and would have liked to sit down. Instead she followed him across the narrow strip of lawn to the edge of the pathless copse. The floor of the wood was fragrant and moist with the humidity of summer; the leaves sighed in the slight wind.

"You are very grave this afternoon," he remarked, when they had proceeded a little ways.

She smiled, forcing herself. "I was thinking . . ."

"Thinking?" he echoed, kissing the top of her head.

"Yes; thinking how little we have to say to one another. I do not know you at all, Christian. Tell me what your family is, where you were born, how you came to be what you are."

"I am always astonished at the interest of women in such things," said he.

"How many others have asked you?" she demanded in spite of herself.

"Ah, that I will not say." He smiled down at her. "Enough to know how to appreciate you; that is all."

She considered this for a moment. "I suppose I must be satisfied with that," she said at last. "Christian, how very odd it is! Every other word you say grates upon me. I do not think we share a single principle—and yet I know you do have principles . . . don't you?"

He laughed. "Still uncertain? Of course I have principles," he said. "I never force myself upon any one; I never condemn any person whom I believe to be sincere; I take every one at his word, but act only upon his behaviour; I accept, in so far as I am able, every good thing which any one presents to me; and I never speak to one lady of another. All that on principle."

She had listened to every word, but it was the last bit of his code which interested her most. "I suppose you would not marry me if you could," she said calmly. "Tell me the truth; it will make no difference, but I must know."

"You have not forgot Madame des Fimes, have you?" he said shrewdly.

"No I have not," she cried. "Christian, what is she to you?"

"How pretty you look, with the sunlight dappling your hair," he replied. He caught at her wrists and she tried to pull away. For some minutes they struggled, almost in earnest but always with the consciousness that it was better to struggle with one another than to agree with any one else. At last Daphne found herself backed up against an oak, the bark rough on her bare shoulders. Christian had got hold of her wrists again, and he held her hands above her head, pinned against the tree. He kissed her mouth.

"I thought you never forced yourself on any one?" she said, when she could speak.

"I must have lied," he answered.

"Christian, you are abominable!"

"And you incorrigible. Now promise that if I let you go you will put your fair arms round me and embrace me for what I am. I feel like a satyr chasing a nymph, and it is very humiliating."

It was difficult for her to do so, but she promised. He released her wrists and she put her arms round him, kissing his neck despondently and hearing his heart beat again. "What are you drawn to in me?" she asked at length.

He paused before speaking. "A different honesty than my own," he said finally. "We will do very well together."

"I think we will quarrel all the time," said she.

"That is precisely what I mean."

They stood together a little while longer, drifting gradually into accord. Daphne left the copse first and walked back through the gardens to the Abbey. Christian followed a few moments later, and returned to the pianoforte. The celebration was to begin at nine.

Chapter X

"Mesdames, Messieurs," called Sir Andrew Ballard loudly from the improvised platform on which he stood, "my good friends, my dear family—a word." He paused to smile benignly as the assembled company quieted, until there was only a low murmur heard here and there. Some hundred persons were present in the enormous Hall, which had once served as the monks' refectory, and had now been converted to a sort of ball-room. To command their attention even for a moment was a feat, but Sir Andrew was accustomed to command, and had that confidence in his public speaking which belongs to all men who are inflated with self-consequence. "First, I must reiterate the welcome which, though I have tried to convey it to each of you severally, yet flows through my grateful and delighted consciousness tonight with such a warmth and a sincerity—and, I may almost say, a passion—that I am obliged, though I fear to presume yet once more on your patience, to speak it again when I find you all standing, with such evident kindness and good-will, gathered before me. The occasion which brings us all together, as you must all know by now—and if you do not, I hasten to tell you—is one of two-fold gladness to me, my Lady, and our friends—among whom, I trust, I may number all of you, as well as so many more good people who, though I am certain their absence tonight pains them as much as it does me, could not join us here—and the sort of events which happen once, and once only I am afraid, in a young life-time, and must therefore be celebrated both with joy at their actuality and regret at their fleeting nature—which is, moreover, the nature of all good things in this sorrowful, yet joyous, world. A foreign gentleman of my acquaintance—and who, perhaps, is among the acquaintance of certain of the kind and illustrious persons assembled here, yet whose name I shall omit to mention, since he is a man of reserved, even humble, disposition, and would doubtless desire to remain anonymous—once remarked to me, with that brevity, precision, and directness which belongs alone to the Frenchman—and I do disclose that he is French, yet say no more of his identity—that the moment of a boy's coming into his majority, of his attaining manhood and ceasing to be a child, of that turning-point when he is no longer protected, but protects, no longer receives, but gives, no longer is governed, but governs, is, or might well be considered (since few other occasions can boast such a variety of crucial and irrevocable transformations) the single most noteworthy, most advantageous, to himself and to his society, in fine, the most important achievement of all his young life.'' There was a rustle among the company as they stirred, and the restless murmur of voices grew somewhat louder. Sir Andrew prosed on in this way for a good half-hour, during which time no one understood, or even attempted to understand, a word that he said; in fact the Hall was so large, and the murmur of the audience grew to such a pitch, that a large portion of the enforced listeners could not have heard him if they had wanted to. Of course, nobody did particularly want to, so it hardly mattered.

The celebration was roundly judged to have been a great success—with the exception, that is, of Sir Andrew's wordy oration. Mr. Livingston played perfectly, as always, and the dancing went on well past three o'clock in the morning. Lady Ballard, whose entertainments in London were generally agreed to be exquisite gems of hospitality, was felt by most of the guests to have outdone even herself: the sweets served after supper were delectable cakes of marchpane, fashioned skilfully into the shapes of various fruits, as delicious to look upon as to taste. Sir Andrew produced, from his capacious cellars, a Spanish sherry sweet and smooth as nectar, and the guests drank, supped, and danced until they could do so no more. Those who lived nearby enough to travel to their homes that evening began to depart at about one o'clock, but the visitors who were to stop the whole night were many, and the Abbey was not silent until five. Lady Ballard was extremely satisfied with herself—with good cause, for once—when she set her competent head to her silken pillow.

Lord Midlake had been called upon to make a speech at supper, and had done so with mumbling good-humour, and convenient terseness. India kept close by him all night, promising herself that she should never do so again once their wedding was behind them, and even pulled teasingly upon his left ear several times. All his younger brothers had come, and none had had the daring to dislike her openly, so she judged herself well on her way to a life of liberal pleasure and easy serenity. William had played his role with perfect form, and had acquitted himself admirably. The nuptials which he hoped to share with Daphne were not referred to publicly, but he did find time and place to approach her privately on that head. She had left the improvised ball-room to catch her breath in the library, which had no official function that evening and was consequently empty of people. She had vague hopes that Christian might find a means to follow her—though she knew this was unlikely, since supper was over and he would be expected to play continuously now. Still, when she heard some one enter the library behind her, her heart leapt a little inside her; turning, she was something more than merely disappointed to find it was William Ballard who had seen her slip away, and had pursued.

"I hope I do not intrude, Miss Keyes," he said with a low bow.

"No; of course you do not."

"You are weary of dancing?" he asked.

"Yes—a little—the incessant noise and movement . . ." Her voice trailed off.

He sat beside her on the full, round-shouldered sofa which stood before the rows of high, book-lined shelves. "I have endeavoured to keep away from you," he said, "so that you might consider my offer in peace; but you must know how difficult it is for me. I would not have you believe that I avoid you for any other reason."

"No," she replied, with a tired smile.

"It has been so long, so long! since we have been alone together."

Daphne murmured agreement, supposing that it must have seemed a long while to him, though it was all too recent for her. "I know you dislike to be pressed, my dear one," he continued in a whisper, "but the celebration is yet in progress . . . if only you could answer me tonight, think how the announcement would perfect the festivity of the evening!"

Daphne noticed that he still assumed her reply would be in the affirmative, but she said nothing. Sitting there in the dark, quiet library, with Christian so close to her and yet so painfully inaccessible, hearing William's proposal repeated so coaxingly—a proposal which, if accepted and consummated, would free her to know Christian as she wished to know him—she thought for a moment, and for the first time, of accepting him. It would not be so terrible:

the marriage might be accomplished quickly; William's amorous fever to possess her would be cooled as soon as she became his wife; the honeymoon would suffice to convince him of their fundamental differences; and then . . . a town-house in London with Christian living nearby; discreet rendez-vous in unfrequented places; William in love with another girl, an actress perhaps, younger and less familiar than herself . . . it was possible. For the first time her imagination grasped it as distinctly possible— and yet some part of her shrank from it. She shook her head, smiled dolefully, and said, "Not yet."

"No?" cried he. "Then I must wait longer. I am all patience in service to you; you see, I do not push."

"You are very good, sir," she replied. It was odd: in an oblique manner, she felt it was true. He *was* very good, only very foolish; he lived a dream and invited her into it. She felt a beginning of tenderness towards him, and did not resent his presumptuousness so much. A moment later she rose to return to the company; he stood too, bestowed a kiss upon her hand, and escorted her back to the great Hall.

Carwaith Abbey did not return to its habitual serenity for many days. Though most of the guests took their leave the following day, a number of them lingered on. Among the latter were Lord and Lady Frane, Lady Ballard's cousin Clarissa, two or three of Midlake's numerous brothers, and of course Mr. Christian Livingston. The original house-party stopped on too, and he performed for them nearly every evening as well as some afternoons, filling the Abbey with Handel, with Scarlatti, with Mozart, and with himself. Daphne listened by the hour to the sweet, sober, ceaseless music—listened while Lady Ballard poured tea as the twilight gathered, while Dorothea Frane murmured pretty nonsense to her betrothed during the long evenings, while responding with half a mind to some question of Latimer's. Now and then Christian would interrupt his absent gaze at the French doors and the velvet hangings to glance at her, meeting her eyes with dreamy languor. The mid-summer days floated past one by one, filled with walks, and riding, and drives to pretty prospects and interesting churches, until almost a se'ennight had gone by since the great celebration. William Ballard had not repeated his offer since then, but Daphne felt he would soon, and she began to think of leaving—though it meant the end of the brief, intimate interchanges she shared almost daily with Christian. She suggested departure tentatively to her brother, who said that he was content either to go or to stay, and so the idyllic interlude drifted on.

It was interrupted with a rude jolt by a letter.

Dome House, in Berkeley Square, London, was about to close its doors for a long, long time—though Daphne did not know it yet. The knocker had already been removed from the front entry-way, and its proprietess stood in the middle of the drawing-room, one hot July morning, reading over a note she had just written. Satisfied that it expressed what she intended, she folded, sealed, and handed it to a footman to be sent. The furniture amid which she stood was shrouded in Holland; the fireplace had been swept bare and its brass fixtures gleamed dully; the carpets had been rolled up and the hangings removed to prevent their fading. When Hastings entered the room, as he did a moment later, she took his arm and—looking round one last time to be certain all was as it should be—descended the front steps of Dome House into an unlozenged coach laden with baggage.

"Is Madam quite ready?" Hastings inquired through a window on the coach.

"Madam is quite ready," she said, with a decisive nod of her powdered head, and an utterly delicious smile.

"Then by all means, let us be off at once," said he. He gave an appropriate command to the boy who held the heads of the horses, climbed into the carriage himself, and sat back as the coachman drove out into the street.

That last letter which had been sent from Dome House was directed to Daphne at Carwaith Abbey. It arrived next morning during breakfast, and was handed to her while the house-party lingered over cool cups of coffee and debated what to do.

"My God!" cried Daphne, just as Charles Stickney was about to suggest a pic-nic at Stove Hill. "Who would ever have believed it?"

"Believed what?" asked Latimer. "What is it?"

Speechless, she waved the letter and let it fall from her hand. Her brother took it up, and in a moment he too cried out. "Well, damme if that ain't doing it a bit too brown!"

"What news is this?" asked everyone at once. "Nothing ill, I hope," said Lady Ballard.

"It is—well, I hardly know what to call her," said Daphne, looking for help at Latimer.

"Our great-grandmother, in any case."

"Yes, indeed. Our great-grandmother. She says she has—that is, she writes to tell me . . ."

"Perhaps you do not like to tell the news aloud," Lord Frane suggested diplomatically. "If it is of a private nature———"

"O no! That is, it is indeed, but every one will know it soon enough, I think. How can she have done it? She has gone off—she has gone off and married her butler!"

"Her butler?" cried every one together. "Shocking! Scandalous! Infamous! Whatever made her do so?" was heard all round.

Daphne blushed crimson for her great-grandmother's behaviour, and so did Latimer. "Apparently, she makes no secret of it," she went on, in deep embarrassment.

"She and Hastings were wed by special licence three days ago, and she held a reception afterwards to which she invited every body, or so it seems. O, I cannot believe it!"

"Perhaps you ought to read the whole letter to us, so we may make some sense of this," said Lord Frane. He felt quite sorry for the poor girl, and hoped to stifle the uproar.

It was Latimer who read it to the company, however. " 'My dear Daphne,' " it began. " 'I have learnt through your mother of your betrothal to William Ballard, and wish to felicitate you upon showing so much good sense. I knew you would do so after our last meeting, and trust you will be very happy.' "

"Who can have told her such a thing?" Daphne interrupted, glancing with acute discomfort at William. "I know I did not."

Latimer's cheeks paled and he looked at her from behind the letter. "I am afraid I did," he said, in the barest whisper. "O Daphne, I wish you will forgive me. I do not deserve it, I know, but—I did not tell her you were betrothed, exactly; but I did say it looked as if you might be, or some such thing. She must have misunderstood, and now—O my dear sister, I am so sorry! Truly I am!" His consternation and confusion overcame him, and he was silent.

"Please continue to read," said Daphne, in a small voice. "Of course it cannot be helped now; and of course I forgive you."

Latimer glanced gratefully at her and proceeded with the letter. " 'I myself have some rather startling news for you regarding marriages. Mr. Hastings and I were married by special licence yesterday, following which we gave a large reception for my London friends. While it is true that not one of them came—excepting my dear Lord Houghton—we had an excellent time and I am enjoying myself thoroughly. You, who are about to embark upon a life in Society, probably cannot appreciate the exquisite delight with which I now bid it adieu. I did not care to do so until I know you safely betrothed, but now . . . My scandalous revenge upon the *ton*—that horde of gossip-mongers, addlepates, and boors who have for sixty years and more scrutinised, criticised, and bored me past bearing—will no doubt be forgot by the time Latimer is ready to marry. By that time we may have returned, though I think not——

" 'But I anticipate myself. I have not yet mentioned that Mr. Hastings and myself are on the point of leaving for what I hope will be an extremely protracted journey to the continent of Africa. From there we shall go on to the Orient, and from there—I do not know.

" 'My dear, words cannot express how happy I am upon this occasion. I can only say that I have never felt younger or better in my life, and hope that Society agrees with your disposition better than it did with mine. You will convey the contents of this letter to your family, I know. Of all people in the world, I hope that you will not judge me too harshly . . . On second thought, I shall not be much distressed if you do, so go ahead. Much happiness to you and William. I am etc., etc.'

"She signs it Mrs. Clyde Hastings," Latimer added, as he came to the end of the missive, "with Countess of Halston in parentheses afterwards."

For several minutes after he had done, no one said a word. Every one's dismay was evident, however, and eventually the table broke out anew in a chorus of Shocking! and Scandalous! "I beg you will excuse us," Daphne said at last, rising and taking Latimer with her. Sir Andrew rose at the same time, to talk to his son in the library. Lady Ballard was hard put to restore order to the table, and the buzz of speculation and reaction continued for a long while.

Miss Keyes had led the way directly to her bedchamber, where she and Latimer sat—mostly in silence—trying to understand what had happened. When they had been there for an hour or so, India Ballard's knock was heard at the door, and she entered looking quite pale.

"My dear Daphne," she said, rushing to her friend and taking her hand. "How mortified you must be!"

Daphne nodded agreement.

"How can she have done it? That selfish old woman . . . I should like to murder her myself."

"I suppose . . . if she hated Society as much as she said——" Daphne began feebly.

"Yes, but after all! What is left of your prospects now? This scandal will not die down for years—and you will be quite old by then! It is utterly outrageous."

"She could always marry William," Latimer suggested doubtfully.

But here India blushed deep scarlet. "O no . . . I am afraid she could not." She held her friend's hand in both her own and almost knelt before her. "Daphne—my dearest Daphne—I am afraid . . . William will not offer for you again. My father has forbidden him to do so. I know it must sound terribly cruel to you—and, indeed, it is not very kind—but our name in Society is simply not so well established that we can afford . . . that is, even I am forced to confess . . . and then, what Midlake would say . . . You see how it is, do not you?"

Daphne's head ached extremely, but she was beginning to understand her own, altered circumstances. "Of course I see," she replied, very slowly. "Certainly, it would not answer to ally oneself to a family so steeped in scandal. No—your father's prohibition is doubtless his wisest, his only, course. You must not be distressed, India."

"William is distressed as well," she said.

Daphne sighed. "He must have been disappointed any way, for I did not mean to accept him."

"Yes; there is that," said India glumly.

Latimer was almost in tears. "How could she?" he exclaimed again. "At least she ought to have waited until Daphne married——"

"But she thought I was betrothed, and she knows no gentleman would break off a betrothal no matter what the circumstances," Miss Keyes interrupted. "Well, I suppose there is nothing for it but to go down-stairs among the others and face them bravely. We will be looked upon askance for a long time to come, and we must become accustomed to it." Her tone was resolved, but her face was drawn and colourless.

"I think," said India, very timidly indeed, "I think—perhaps it would be easiest for you . . . best for all of us, I suppose I mean, if——" Her voice faded to silence.

Daphne stared at her. "You mean we ought to leave. Yes," she went on flatly, "you are quite right. It would be the worst behaviour to stay on and overset everybody. Will this afternoon be soon enough?"

"If it were only myself——" India began faintly.

"Yes, I know it is not you, dear. Your mother must be very much dismayed . . . it is no wonder. You must assure her we are going directly."

"I am so sorry, truly——" said India, vastly relieved at not being obliged to order her friends away.

"It is nothing, dear, nothing. Will you be a love and see that our carriage is prepared for us? And send Lizzy to me, so I may pack directly?"

India rose. "Certainly," she said. She lingered in the door-way for a moment, as if about to add something but afraid to.

"What is it?" asked Daphne. "Is there——? O,

dinner no doubt. Well, you must send our excuses to Lady Ballard, for we shall be gone before then. Perhaps you might be good enough to send a nuncheon up here about one o'clock. I don't think we shall—have time—to go down-stairs at all.''

"I do love you," India said, and hastened from the room.

Daphne turned to her brother. "Well, we have a great deal to do, and not much time. It wants about fifteen minutes till noon, I should think, so go and pack your things."

"As you say," he agreed. "I'll come back here as soon as I've done, so we may eat together."

"That will be very pleasant." She smiled and nudged him towards the door. When he had gone she sat upon her bed and wept, more from confusion than from shame. Fifteen minutes later, Lizzy arrived to help her pack, and she went on with her arrangements efficiently and dry-eyed.

They left the Abbey at two, Latimer's man arranging their valises in the coach. Neither of them had ventured down-stairs again, except when they departed. Dorothea Frane had hovered in Daphne's doorway for a moment, and whispered, "I'm sorry," very sweetly indeed. Sir Andrew and Lady Ballard said good-bye to them on the Abbey's broad porch, receiving their thanks as if nothing unusual had happened, but other than these three—and India of course—they saw no one all day. It was not until their carriage was rolling down the drive that Daphne remembered Christian; she realized that he must have been with the others, and that it would have looked very odd if he had insisted on saying good-bye. How the news had affected him she could not guess; she knew at least that it would be a long time before they met again, and tried to feel relieved at not having to face him. She did not succeed very well.

The surprise of Sir Latimer and Lady Keyes at the unexpected arrival of their children may be easily imagined. Their delight in seeing them again was soon offset by the extraordinary tidings they brought. Lady Keyes could not cease exclaiming for hours: she was more dismayed, it seemed, by the Ballards' heavy-handed treatment of her offspring than by any thing else, and Sir Latimer patted her back and said "there, there" all evening. Mr. Clayton was called in to be informed of the news, and to give his opinion of how, if at all, Lady Bryde's estate would be affected by her marriage. Mr. Clayton did not think there would be any change, unless Lady Bryde—Mrs. Hastings, rather—had gone so mad as to change her will, in addition to her other follies. In that case, it was possible her fortune might be settled on her husband; however, it was sure to revert to the Keyes family eventually. Mr. Clayton, though he did not mention it, was very glad this evening; in fact, he was the only member of the household who was. His gladness arose, of course, from the fact that Miss Keyes was not betrothed after all. Unfortunately for him, this source of contentment was short-lived in the extreme.

Verchamp Park received a caller on the day following Daphne's and Latimer's flight from Carwaith. The caller, as it happened, had also just come from the Abbey. Lady Keyes received him in the drawing-room, and thought it very odd that he should come. She complied with his request, however, that he be allowed to speak to Miss Keyes; and when that lady had come down, he invited her to walk with him on the wide lawn of the Park. Clover, bounding delightedly, accompanied them.

"I am sure you should not have come, Christian," she

said (for he it was who called), as they strolled over the green slopes. "It will give a very singular appearance, should any one find out about it."

"If I am fortunate enough," said he, "every one will find out about it."

"I beg your pardon?"

"Miss Keyes, would you do me the great honour to become my wife?"

"I beg your pardon?" she repeated.

"Naturally, I would become your husband as well," he continued.

"But how——"

"Well, we should be obliged to get married first, of course."

"Christian, what is all this madness?" she demanded.

"My love," he answered, stopping and holding her still before him, "have you not yet perceived how your great-grandmother's marriage will affect us? When the Countess of Halston marries her butler, no one will even think twice about her great-grand-daughter wedding a pianofortist."

"But my dear——!" said she.

"If there is no way to reconcile your parents," he went on, "in spite of all that has happened, then we must elope. However, I certainly should prefer it if——"

"My parents will have very little objection, I think," she interrupted, "when I tell them how it is. It was the Countess herself who insisted on my making an advantageous match. But you refused to elope with me!"

"I refused when your name was unsullied by scandal," he protested. "As things stand now, I doubt that Society could be any crueller to you than it means to be already. I have seen the sins of the father visited upon the sons too many times to imagine that the sins of your great-grandmother will not be visited upon you. You saw yourself what happened at Carwaith Abbey," he added cynically. "I assure you, no one mentioned your name, once you had gone, except to heap disapproval upon it."

"Did they?" she cried. "How—O, how awful."

"Not Miss Ballard," he amended kindly. "She did not mention your name at all. Very wise of her, too, since her mother would have boxed her ears."

"Then I had no defenders?"

"None, I am afraid," he said gently. "That is—except myself. I should think it would be some years before any member of the English *ton* engaged my services again," he smiled, musing.

"O, my poor Christian!" she exclaimed. "Your career——"

"A career playing contre-dances in overcrowded ballrooms was never quite what I envisioned any way," he said. "Believe me, the sort of gentlemen who arrange concerts in Europe are not the fellows to be dismayed by the information that their pianofortist has a noble English wife—be her great-grandmother ever so disreputable."

"Then——" Daphne began, and paused. A breeze, lightly scented with the faintest hint of autumn, was blowing across the lawn. It ruffled her heavy curls and brushed her neck deliciously. "Christian," she said at last, putting her arms round him and looking up into his luminous green eyes, "are we really going to Europe?"

"For as long as we like, my love," he answered. "Until all the many scandals of the Keyes family are too stale to mention, if we wish. I too had a letter at Carwaith yesterday, and there is a Viennese opera-manager who awaits my answer eagerly. So to oblige him, I really think we ought to be married as soon as possible—if you do not mind."

"O my dear," she said, feeling almost dizzy with surprise and happiness, "I never believed you would marry me."

"Neither did I," he confessed, as his arms slipped round her to complete their embrace. "It is shocking to admit it—but neither did I."

HISTORICAL NOVELS
BY FIONA HILL

THE TRELLISED LANE	(N2794—95¢)
THE WEDDING PORTRAIT	(N2857—95¢)
THE PRACTICAL HEART	(N2922—95¢)

BY GEORGETTE HEYER

ARABELLA	(Z2181—$1.25)
APRIL LADY	(Z2228—$1.25)
SYLVESTER	(D2995—$1.50)

Send for a *free* list of all our books in print

These books are available at your local bookstore, or send price indicated plus 25¢ per copy to cover mailing costs to Berkley Publishing Corporation, 200 Madison Avenue, New York, N.Y. 10016.

ROMANCES BY
ANNE DUFFIELD

THE GOLDEN SUMMER	(N2500—95¢)
COME BACK MIRANDA	(Z2971—$1.25)
FOREVER TOMORROW	(Z2672—$1.25)
FIAMETTA	(Z2702—$1.25)
THE GRAND DUCHESS	(Z2726—$1.25)

Send for a *free* list of all our books in print

These books are available at your local bookstore, or send price indicated plus 25¢ per copy to cover mailing costs to Berkley Publishing Corporation, 200 Madison Avenue, New York, N.Y. 10016.